RA...
STREET
PETS

WENDY
ORR

ALLEN&UNWIN
SYDNEY · MELBOURNE · AUCKLAND · LONDON

CONTENTS

For all the animals, from Frieda to Harry,
who have enriched my life.

WENDY ORR

First published in 2012

Allen & Unwin
83 Alexander Street, Crows Nest NSW 2065, Australia
Phone: (61 2) 8425 0100, Fax: (61 2) 9906 2218
Email: info@allenandunwin.com, Web: www.allenandunwin.com

A Cataloguing-in-Publication entry is available from
the National Library of Australia — www.trove.nla.gov.au

ISBN 978 174237 908 1

Cover and text design by Bruno Herfst
Cover photos by iStockphoto and Can Stock Photo
Set in 12 pt Sabon by Toolbox
Printed and bound in Australia by Griffin Press

7 9 10 8 6

Lost Dog Bear

CHAPTER 1

hat Bear liked best, almost more than anything in the world, was riding in the back of the ute. He liked racing from side to side to see everything whooshing past, sniffing the wind as it ruffled his fur, and barking at dogs on the ground.

The other thing Bear liked best, almost more than anything in the world, was bossing sheep and making them go where he wanted.

What he liked best of all, more than anything else in the world, was Lachlan – because Lachlan was his boy.

What Lachlan liked best, almost more than anything in the world, was riding around the farm in the back of the ute. He liked bouncing over the bumps, singing into the wind as it ruffled his hair, and watching Bear race from side to side. He liked the way his friends from town thought riding in the back with him was as cool as all the things they did in town.

The other thing Lachlan liked best, almost more than anything in the world, was walking around the farm with his dad and watching Bear herd the sheep wherever his dad wanted them to go.

What he liked best of all, more than anything else in the world, was Bear – because Bear was his dog.

But now Lachlan's mother and father had sold the farm. His dad and Bear were going to work on a big sheep farm, and Lachlan and his mum were moving to the city. Lachlan felt as if he was being pulled in two.

'Your dad and I are still friends,' said his mum. 'We just can't live together anymore.'

'It doesn't change how I feel about you,' said his dad. 'I still love you as much as ever.'

'But what about Bear?' asked Lachlan. 'How's he supposed to understand?'

'He'll like it there,' said his dad. 'They have a couple of working dogs already – Bear will get along fine with them.'

'He'll hate it!' shouted Lachlan. 'He'll miss me!'

His dad pulled Lachlan close and hugged him. 'Not as much as I'll miss you,' he said. 'But maybe you're right. Maybe Bear should go with you.'

'The yard in our new house is very small,' said Lachlan's mum.

'I'll walk him every day,' said Lachlan. 'Bear won't care where he lives, as long as he's with me.'

What Hannah liked best, almost more than anything in the world, was going to the beach. She liked diving through the waves with her friends, and racing along the sand with her ponytail flying in the wind.

But what Hannah liked more than anything was dogs. And what she wanted, more than absolutely anything else in the world, was a dog of her own.

'Our garden's not big enough,' said her dad.

'I'd walk it every day,' said Hannah.

'Dogs get smelly!' said her mum.

'I'd give it a bath,' said Hannah.

'You'd forget to feed it,' said her dad.

'I'd *never* forget,' said Hannah.

Every time The Coopers went to Hannah's friend Ellie's house, they passed a narrow street with a sign shaped like an arrow, saying RAINBOW STREET SHELTER. And every time Hannah asked, 'Could we go there?'

'It would just make you sad,' said her mum. 'You'd want to bring home a dog.'

'I already want to bring home a dog,' Hannah pointed out. 'And I wouldn't be sad if I could.'

But her mother always sighed, 'Oh, Hannah!' and drove on.

The moving van came early in the morning. The moving men packed up all the boxes and furniture that Lachlan and his mum were taking to their new house. They left the boxes and furniture that Lachlan's dad was taking to his new home.

Lachlan tried to hug his dad so tight that he'd have to get in the car with them, and his dad hugged him back so tight that Lachlan felt like a quivery jelly – but his dad still said goodbye.

Then Lachlan and Bear got into the car, and his mum drove away. Bear stuck his head out the window and barked. Lachlan stuck his head out the other window and waved till he couldn't see his house or his father anymore.

It was a hot, dry day, and the dust from the long farm driveway drifted in the car windows.

His mum sneezed. 'Roll up your window,' she said.

'I like the dust!' said Lachlan.

He rolled the window up, but he left a good wide crack at the top to let a little more of the farm's earth blow in and go with them to the city.

Lachlan had been to the city before, but it had never seemed as far as it did today. The car had never been so hot, and Bear had never raced so excitedly back and forth across the seat. He stood on Lachlan's bare legs with his sharp nails.

'Ouch, Bear!'

Bear leaned against him and drooled down Lachlan's neck.

'Yuck, Bear!'

Bear licked Lachlan's legs.

'Don't lick, Bear!' shouted Lachlan, and shoved him away.

Bear twisted around and licked Lachlan's

hands instead. Lachlan's dad always joked that Bear thought 'Don't lick, Bear!' was his full name.

'Maybe you should have gone with Dad, Bear,' said Lachlan.

At lunchtime, Lachlan and his mum stopped at Terri's Takeaway. It was across the road from a wide sandy beach with crashing, blue surf – but dogs weren't allowed on the beach. So they parked in the shade, and Lachlan walked Bear around the edge of the car park. It was the first time Bear had ever been on a leash, but he walked beside Lachlan as if he were a guide dog, watching all the people and cars and sniffing the strange new smells.

Even when they got back to the car and Bear was drinking his bowl of water, he kept stopping every few seconds to stare around.

'Now he'll be fresh to start licking again,' Lachlan's mum teased as she opened the door to the back seat.

Bear hopped in and Lachlan rolled the window down so Bear could sniff the fresh air. Then Lachlan and his mum went into the cafe. Lachlan looked out at the ocean, and for the first time since he'd found out they were moving, he felt a sparkle of happiness.

'Are we going to live near a beach?' he asked as they walked back to the car after lunch.

'Pretty close,' said his mum. 'Too far to walk, but a short drive.'

'Could I ride my bike?'

'When you're older,' said his mum.

The sparkle fizzed and died. Lachlan didn't want to be older in their new house. He didn't want to have a birthday without his dad. He wanted to pretend they were just going to the beach for this last weekend of summer holidays, and would be back in their old home when school started again.

His eyes blurred as he got into the car, and he squeezed them tight so that no tears could sneak through. His mum pulled out onto the highway, and they started down the coast towards their new home.

'How long till we get there?' he asked.

'About an hour,' said his mum.

Lachlan opened his eyes and wiggled back in his seat. He reached over for Bear – and suddenly the hot day turned cold.

'Mum,' he said, 'where's Bear?'

CHAPTER 3

Bear was not in the car park. Lachlan and his mum raced around, shouting Bear's name and looking everywhere a dog could possibly hide. They asked everyone in the cafe and the playground and the petrol station next door.

No one had seen a lost dog.

'Maybe he went to the beach,' said Lachlan.

'He couldn't have crossed the highway,' said his mum. 'It's too busy. It's more likely he tried to follow us when we left.'

She drove slowly down the road to where Lachlan had realised Bear was gone. Cars honked behind them, but all Lachlan and his mother cared about was finding Bear.

There was no lost dog running along the side of the highway.

'He might have tried to head for home,' said his mum, and turned around again. She drove back towards the farm until they knew they'd gone further than Bear could have possibly run.

There was no lost dog heading towards his old home.

'We should check the beach just in case,' said Lachlan's mum, and turned around again.

They parked right across from Terri's Takeaway and ran down a path to the beach.

'Bear!' shouted Lachlan.

'Here, Bear!' shouted his mum.

Their voices were small against the noise of the waves and the people shouting and playing. There were surfers carrying surfboards to the water or peeling off their wetsuits; there were families setting up beach umbrellas or having picnics; there were little kids splashing in the shallows or building sandcastles, bigger kids on boogie boards or playing frisbee, grandparents taking pictures.

'BEAR!' roared Lachlan.

The people nearby turned to stare.

'Not a real bear,' explained Lachlan's mum. 'A dog named Bear.'

'Because he looked like a bear cub when he was a puppy,' said Lachlan. 'But now he's lost! Here, Bear!'

They ran from one group of people to the next, asking if anyone had seen a shaggy black border collie with a crooked white stripe down his face, a white neck and three white paws.

No one had.

'It's no good, Lachlan,' said his mum. 'He couldn't have crossed the highway.'

Lachlan followed his mum along the beach. His stomach was swirling sickly, but he knew Bear would be feeling worse.

Three boys jogged past.

'Have you seen a lost dog?' Lachlan called.

'A big black dog?'

Lachlan tried to say yes, but only a small choking sound came out. He nodded.

'He was running that way!'

'About twenty minutes ago!'

Suddenly Lachlan could breathe again. 'Thanks!' he shouted.

Lachlan and his mum raced back the way they'd

come, kicking through the soft white sand till they couldn't run anymore and had to stop, doubled over and gasping to catch their breath.

They were at the path to the highway.

There was no black dog.

Lachlan and his mother swerved down to the hard wet sand where the tide had gone out and started to run again. *We've got to see him soon!* Lachlan thought, and shouted as he ran, 'Here, Bear!'

They passed a family wading in the shallows.

'Have you seen a lost dog?'

'Sorry,' said the dad, 'we've just got here.'

Lachlan and his mum ran on. Their faces were red, their T-shirts were wet with sweat, and their chests were hurting.

They asked two girls reading on their towels. The girls hadn't seen a dog all morning.

Neither had a boy splashing in from the surf with his board.

But a mum tidying up a picnic said, 'He was here about fifteen minutes ago.'

'I gave him a sausage roll,' said her little boy.

'He went that way,' said the mum. She pointed back the way Lachlan and his mum had just run.

CHAPTER 4

Hannah came up with such a wonderful idea that her ponytail quivered.

If her parents didn't have the time to take care of a dog, there might be other people who already had a dog and didn't have time to take care of it either. They must need someone to take their dog for walks and play with it.

She got out some paper and markers. She printed HANNAH THE DOG-WALKER on the top. She drew paw prints underneath and put her phone number at the bottom.

'You can't do that!' her mum exclaimed. 'It's not safe to put your phone number up on posters everywhere.'

'I could take it to the Rainbow Street Shelter,' said Hannah. 'They could give it to people who want a dog but can't take it for walks.'

'Hannah!' her mother sighed. 'You are *not* going to the animal shelter. I don't want to talk about it any more.'

Lachlan and his mum ran up and down the beach for three hours. The only times they stopped were to gulp down water and ask if anyone had seen a lost black dog.

'Ten minutes ago,' said someone.

'He was just here,' said someone else.

'Half an hour ago,' said a third.

They all pointed in different directions.

A girl smearing on sunscreen pointed to the path above the beach.

A mother pushing a toddler on a swing pointed back down.

A man packing up his sailboat pointed to the place where they had starred.

This way and that way and back again Lachlan

and his mother ran, kicking through sand, pushing through people, calling and looking. Finally it was so late that the beach wasn't crowded anymore, and they knew that if Bear was anywhere around they'd be able to see him, and he would see them. And when they couldn't, they knew that Bear wasn't anywhere they'd been looking.

'I'm sorry, Lachlan,' said his mum. 'We have to go on to the house. I'll figure out what to do when we get there.'

'Maybe they all saw some other dog,' said Lachlan. 'A dog who liked the beach.'

All the time they'd been running up and down the beach, Bear had been lost and frightened somewhere else – and now they might never find him.

Lachlan couldn't stop wishing he'd never pushed Bear away and told him he should have gone with Dad after all.

Hannah had been in a grumpy mood ever since her mum had said she couldn't go to the Rainbow Street Shelter. Her ponytail moped around the back of her neck. She couldn't think of anything she wanted to do.

Now the grumpiness dissolved like an icy pole on the pavement.

Her dad was coming home from work: he was driving into the driveway and parking in the carport just like he always did. There was just one thing different.

In the back of his ute was a dog.

CHAPTER 5

he dog was black and furry, with a crooked white stripe down his face, a white neck and three white paws.

'What's that dog doing there?' Hannah's mum demanded.

'*What?* How did that dog get there?' her dad said.

'Hannah!' they shouted together. 'Get down from there!'

But Hannah was already in the back of the ute with her arms around the dog, and the dog was licking her face. His tongue was warm, wet and tickly, and he was panting fast as if he was excited.

Hannah jumped down from the ute and threw her arms around her father. 'Thank you, thank you, *thank you*!' she squealed.

'But Hannah–' her dad began.

'We can't keep it,' said her mum.

Hannah didn't hear. She ran inside to get a bowl of water for the thirsty dog. The dog jumped down after her, waiting at the front door till she came out. Hannah patted him while he drank big splashing gulps with his long red tongue.

'He's so soft,' she told her parents. 'And so nice. I'm going to call him Surprise, because he was the biggest surprise I ever got.'

'Me too,' said her dad. 'He must have jumped into the wrong ute when we went home.'

'He's got to go back to where he came from,' said her mum.

'As soon as we can figure out where that is!' said her dad.

'Were there many dogs where you were working today?' asked her mum.

'A few.'

Hannah's dad phoned everyone he worked with, but the answer was always the same: no one had lost their dog. No one had even seen a stray dog.

Nobody wants him! thought Hannah. *Nobody except me!* She ran into the shed to find a piece of rope, and looped it through the ring on the dog's collar. There was a metal tag on the ring.

'D L Bear,' Hannah read in a small voice. 'And there's a phone number.'

Her dad got out his phone again and tried the number.

'It's been disconnected – it's lucky they put their name on the tag too, so we can try to find them.'

'Imagine how worried they must be!' said her mum.

Hannah didn't want to imagine, but she did. She imagined them like Papa Bear, Mama Bear and Baby Bear, except instead of porridge they'd be saying, 'Who's been taking my dog?'

She didn't want to be Goldilocks.

'And just think how happy they'll be when we give the dog back,' said her dad. 'We *have* to find them.'

But there were no new phone numbers for Bears anywhere in the whole state.

'So we'll have to look after Surprise,' said Hannah. 'At least until we find the Bears.'

Surprise pricked his ears.

'He knows his new name already!' Hannah said. 'He's a really smart dog.'

She tugged the rope. 'Come on, Surprise!' And she led him into the backyard. The dog followed happily.

'See how good he is!' Hannah told her parents. She shut the gate behind her and ran over to the front step for the bowl of water.

Surprise leapt over the fence and up onto the ute.

'No, Surprise!' Hannah whispered, and tried to push him back into the yard before her parents noticed.

It was too late.

'We can't keep him,' said her mum. 'He'll run away again, and this time he might get hurt.'

Lachlan and his mum's new house was in the middle of the city. There were houses beside it, houses across the road and houses behind. The garden was small and the fence was tall.

But all Lachlan cared about was that there was no dog.

He looked in the yard, and he looked back down the road, because Bear was the smartest, fastest dog in the world, and Lachlan almost believed that he might have already found his way to their new home. But even Bear wasn't smart enough to find a house he'd never been to, or fast enough to follow a car down the highway.

Inside, the house was jumbled full of furniture

and boxes. The moving men had put the beds in the bedrooms and the couch in the lounge room, but Lachlan's bedroom was so crammed with boxes he had to scramble from one box to another to get to the window. It could have been fun if he hadn't felt like crying.

Hannah had thought it was the best day of her life, and now it was the worst.

'We'll have to take the dog to the animal shelter,' said her dad. 'They can look after him properly while they find the Bears.'

'*I* can look after him properly!' Hannah wanted to shout – but she didn't, because she'd seen him jump over the fence too.

She sat on the grass with her arms around Surprise's neck for a long, long time. Finally she pushed away and looked into his bright, brown eyes. 'Don't worry: if we can't find the Bears, I'll look after you!'

Surprise licked her face, and they got into the back of the ute.

'It might be easier if Dad went by himself,' said her mum.

'I want to go,' said Hannah. It was the biggest lie she'd ever told, because she didn't want to go at all. She just couldn't let Surprise go without her.

Her dad tied the other end of the rope to a ring in his toolbox, so Surprise had enough room to look around but not enough to jump out. Hannah gave him one more hug and got into the front of the ute between her parents.

When they turned at the sign for the Rainbow Street Shelter, Hannah remembered how much she'd wanted to go there every single time they'd driven past. She'd never thought it would be the saddest day of her life.

Rainbow Street was short, and at the end, surrounded by a tall wire fence, was a big garden with shady trees and green lawns. The building was pale blue, with a rainbow arching above the cheery, cherry-red door.

Hannah knew that Surprise had to go back to the Bear family, and she knew she'd be sad that he couldn't live with her. But this didn't look like a sad place, and for the first time she felt the tiniest sliver of hope that something good could still happen.

The sliver wasn't big enough to stop her eyes being so blurry she could hardly see to untie Surprise's rope. Tears splashed onto her cheeks as he jumped out of the ute and licked her face again. By the time her dad opened the gate and latched it behind them, that golden sliver of hope was so small it was nearly invisible.

But it was still there.

And so when Surprise heard all the other dogs barking and his happy, wagging tail began to droop, Hannah straightened herself up. Her ponytail bounced, and her voice came out stronger than she'd thought it would, like the voice of someone who'd hardly been crying at all.

'Come on, Surprise! It'll be all right.'

CHAPTER 7

The reception area was bright and cheerful. A woman with long dark hair tied up into a knot, and a name-tag that said MONA was working at a computer. A white cockatoo with a crooked left wing was sitting on a perch above the desk, and on the wall behind him was a framed photograph of a lion with three cubs.

'Can I help you?'

It was an old man's voice, deep and gravelly. Hannah stared in amazement, because she couldn't see him anywhere.

'That's Gulliver,' said Mona, pointing to the cockatoo. 'He likes being the receptionist.'

'Gulliver!' repeated the cockatoo.

'We've got a lost dog,' said Mr Cooper.

'Poor little fellow,' said Mona, coming around the other side of the desk to see Surprise. She squatted down beside him and felt him all over while Hannah's dad explained what had happened. A small, brown-and-white dog with a stumpy-tail followed her and sniffed Surprise as if she was checking him too.

'The vet will have a look later, but he seems okay,' Mona said. 'I wonder if he's been micro-chipped?'

She got an electronic wand from her desk and ran it over Surprise's neck and shoulders. There was no beep.

'That's a shame,' Mona sighed. 'Well, let's hope the owners find us. He's a lovely dog.'

Surprise was panting nervously. Hannah put her arm around his neck. Surprise licked her as if he was saying thank you.

'Bert will take him now,' Mona said, as a grey-haired man came in.

'G'day, mate!' said the cockatoo, in his scratchy old-man's voice.

'Say goodbye, Hannah,' said her mum.

But the old man smiled. 'Maybe Hannah would like to see where the dog's going to stay?'

His voice was the same as the cockatoo's.

Hannah nodded.

'Okay,' said Mona and Mrs Cooper.

Hannah kept her hand on Surprise's shoulder as they followed Bert out to the hall. The stumpy-tailed dog trotted back behind the desk, and a grey cat in the windowsill sat up to clean his paws and watch Surprise leave.

There were doors marked EXAMINATION ROOM and SURGERY, and rooms full of cages, some with a dog, cat, rabbit or possum dozing inside.

'That's the hospital for the sick animals,' said Bert. 'But this fella will go out here.' He opened the back door.

There was a big aviary full of birds on one side; behind it was another big enclosure with a tree in the middle and three fat hollow logs scattered around: 'For the wild animals getting ready to be set free again,' said Bert.

Away from the aviary was an enclosure where cats lazed in the sun in front of their own small shelters; there was another enclosure for rabbits. Wooden walls separated them so the cats and bunnies didn't have to see each other, and neither of them had to see the dogs. On the lawn behind them, a three-legged goat was grazing. She looked quite happy, as if she hadn't noticed her hind leg was missing.

Bert opened a gate and they walked through to the dog area.

There was a dusty lawn with two shady trees and a few bushes. The kennels were in a big U around it. Each kennel had its own fenced run; some had one dog, some had two. There were big dogs, short stubby-legged dogs, hairy dogs and smooth. Two in a run together were playing, some of the others were dozing, but most were watching Bert, Hannah and Surprise.

They crossed the lawn to an empty run.

Surprise's tail drooped, and so did his head. He did not want to go into the cage.

Hannah didn't want him to go in either.

'Come on, boy,' Bert coaxed. 'Nobody's going to hurt you.' He opened the door of the run.

Surprise stopped.

Bert tugged gently at his collar.

Surprise stuck his front legs out straight and wouldn't move.

Hannah's eyes filled up with tears. She could hardly see as she walked into the cage and squatted down in front of the kennel.

'Come on, Surprise,' she said, and Surprise walked in.

CHAPTER 8

achlan went through all the boxes till he found some paper and coloured markers. He drew sign after sign saying:

LOST!

BLACK-AND-WHITE BORDER COLLIE
  NAMED BEAR
WITH WHITE STRIPE DOWN HIS FACE
HE BELONGS TO LACHLAN PLEASE PHONE
IF YOU KNOW ANYTHING ABOUT HIM

Their phone wasn't connected yet, so he put his mum's mobile number on the bottom.

He wished he could start putting the posters up

on every street corner, but there was no point – it was impossible for Bear to be anywhere around here. He'd have to wait till tomorrow and go back to the beach.

Hannah and Surprise sat together in front of the kennel and looked around at the other dogs in their runs.

'With a bit of luck, his owner will find him quickly,' said Bert.

Hannah nodded. For the first time, she really did want Surprise's family to find him.

'He seems a friendly boy. If the vet's happy with him, he might let him share a run with another dog.'

Hannah thought Surprise would like that, but not as much as he'd like having his own home.

'And of course he can have a turn in the playground – that's the best part of a volunteer's job.' Bert pointed to the dusty lawn in the middle of the U of kennels. 'We let them out in here to run around, sniff all the new smells, play ball…'

'Do you like playing ball?' Hannah whispered to Surprise, rubbing her tears dry against his shaggy shoulder. The dog pricked his ears.

Bert laughed. 'Okay! As soon as the vet says so, we'll have a game – but you have to be nice to an old man. I reckon you've got more energy than me!'

Hannah's ponytail swished. 'I've got lots of energy,' she said. 'I could come and play with him. And clean his cage and feed him – and *everything*!'

'We'll have to ask your mum and dad,' said Bert.

The Coopers were still talking to Mona at the front desk.

'G'day, mate!' squawked Gulliver.

'I've got an idea,' said Hannah.

'So do we,' said her mum.

Hannah felt a little candle of hope – were they going to let her keep Surprise until his real family found him?

'You know that this dog has to go back to his owners.'

But if they don't want him … Hannah thought.

'And you know that our fence isn't tall enough to keep him in.'

'I'll help you build a bigger one!'

Her dad smiled. 'Our fence will work just fine.'

'Come and see,' said Mum, and Mona led them into a room with small animals in cages.

In the corner was a hutch, and inside it was a fat black guinea pig.

CHAPTER 9

Hannah liked guinea pigs, and this one was very cute. She picked him up and he was warm and soft. She thought about how happy she would have been if she'd met this guinea pig this morning, before she'd met Surprise. She wished she didn't feel like someone at a party who'd got an apple when everyone else had cake.

'Thank you,' she said.

Mona was watching her carefully. 'A guinea pig may be small,' she said, 'but he deserves to be wanted and loved. If you don't feel you can do that, you shouldn't take him.'

Hannah hesitated. The guinea pig wiggled

warmly against her shoulder. 'I'll love him,' she said. 'I'll take him out to eat fresh grass every single day. But I still need to tell you my idea: I want to be a volunteer like Bert.'

'You're not really old enough,' said Mona.

'But I could help him,' said Hannah.

'I'm pretty old,' Bert agreed. 'Mix our ages up together and we'll both come out just right.'

'You'll get upset when the owner comes to pick up this dog,' said Mum.

'No I won't!' said Hannah, but she knew she was lying.

'Only three days till school starts,' said her mum. 'You won't have time to look after the guinea pig properly and come to the shelter.'

'The guinea pig or the shelter,' said Dad. 'Not both.'

'Go home and think about it,' said Mona.

That night, Lachlan squeezed between the boxes and sat on his bedroom floor to talk to his dad on the phone.

'Bear's a smart dog,' his dad said. 'He'll be heading back to the farm. We've just got to figure out where he's got to and start searching there.'

'He'll be so scared.'

'That's why we've got to keep on searching. And hoping.'

CHAPTER 10

In Lachlan's nightmares, sometimes it was Bear that was lost, sometimes it was him and once his dad – but waking up was the worst of all because it was real.

It was very early, but his crammed-full room felt too horribly empty to stay in any longer. He crept quietly through the boxes to the kitchen. His mum was already dressed and studying a map as she drank her coffee.

'I've talked to Dad. He's on his way down to this spot here, fifteen kilometres from where Bear jumped out,' she said, pointing to the map. 'He'll search from there towards the farm, and we'll search from there back down to the beach.'

Lachlan choked down a bowl of cereal, and they left.

In Hannah's dreams, her dad came home with a guinea pig in the back of his ute, and she kept hiding lost dogs in her bedroom – big and little, black, brown, white and spotted, barking, bouncing dogs – till her room was so full she could hardly shut the door.

Hannah couldn't decide if it was a good dream or a nightmare, but now that she was awake she was too happy to care. Her ponytail bounced as she skipped out to the kitchen.

'What have you decided?' asked her mum.

Hannah told her. She choked down a bowl of cereal, and when it was finally nine o'clock, they left.

Mona wasn't at the desk when they got to the Rainbow Street Shelter, but Gulliver was.

'Can I help you?' he asked.

Hannah and her mum laughed, and Mona

came in from the room with the small cages. 'So … are you here for the guinea pig?' she asked.

Hannah shook her head. 'He's a very nice guinea pig,' she said, feeling as mean as if she'd left her best friend out of a secret.

'He is. But you can't take an animal home just because he's nice – you have to know he's the one for you.'

'G'day, mate!' squawked Gulliver, and Bert came in.

'G'day,' he said to the bird. He smiled at Hannah. 'Let's get going, helper!'

Hannah skipped behind him out to the kennels and across to Surprise.

The dog was at the front of his run, and his ears quivered when he saw Hannah and Bert.

'The vet checked him this morning,' Bert said. 'He's good and healthy, just feeling a bit lost.'

'Poor lost Surprise,' said Hannah. 'I hope your family comes soon.'

'We need to give him some breakfast,' said Bert. 'Then we'll clean out his run and give him a turn in the playground.'

He measured out a scoop of dog food from

a big bin. 'Sit!' he said, and the dog sat while Hannah poured the biscuits into his dish.

'Leave him alone while he eats, and we'll feed the others.'

The kennel beside Surprise had a scruffy, shaggy little white dog in it. She was lying inside her kennel, just her nose outside, watching.

'Don't go in,' Bert warned. 'Have a look from here.'

Hannah peeked in from outside the run. Behind the little dog's front legs she could see what looked like a row of fat, squirmy sausage rolls snuggled up to drink from their mother.

'Puppies!' Hannah breathed.

'Five of them,' Bert said. 'Dumped at the gate last week. They're about five weeks old now, so unless someone wants to take the mother and all the puppies, this lot will have to wait another three weeks to go to new homes.'

Very quietly, he took a bowl of breakfast into the run and put it in front of the little dog. 'She's still scared, and she wants to protect her babies from us,' he said. 'She'll bite if she thinks she has to.'

Bert fed the other dogs, and then let Hannah

give a chunky black labrador his biscuits. The labrador was named Sam, and the sign on his cage said, READY TO ADOPT.

'Now your pal can have a turn in the playground while I hose out his run.' Bert clipped a leash onto Surprise's collar and handed it to Hannah.

Hannah shook her head. 'I'll hose,' she said. It didn't seem fair to come to help and only do the fun things. So she hosed the run clean, and then Bert gave her the leash, and Hannah and Surprise ran up and down and all around the playground.

'Come!' Bert called, and when they jogged over to him, he gave Surprise a little piece of dog biscuit.

'Good dog!' said Hannah, because Surprise had gone to Bert himself, even though she'd been at the end of the leash too.

Bert unclipped it, and showed Surprise a red ball.

'Fetch!' he said, as he threw it across the playground.

Surprise shot after it so fast he caught it before it bounced, and then dropped it at their feet. Hannah threw it over and over, and Surprise leapt and bounded from one side of the playground to the other, catching the ball till it was so slippery with slobber she had to wipe it on the grass before she could throw it.

'Hannah!' called her mum. 'Time to go home.'

Hannah hugged Surprise tight, and led him back to his run.

'What about the other dogs?' she asked as she followed Bert out the gate.

'They'll get their turns. But your mate's the youngest – he takes the most running.'

Lachlan and his mum put posters up on street corners for blocks in every direction from Terri's Takeaway. They walked way down the beach where people had seen Bear the day before. They drove around the streets where Bear might have run when he left the beach. They stopped to ask people walking their own dogs.

They never saw Bear, and no one they asked had seen him either.

They phoned all the vets, and went to an

animal shelter full of sad lost dogs, but none of them was Bear.

Lachlan's dad did all the same things going back towards the farm, but he hadn't found Bear either.

'We'll find him,' he said again on the phone. 'Don't give up hope.'

'Just before Bear ran away,' Lachlan whispered, sliding down in his hidey-hole between the bedroom boxes, 'I told him maybe he should have gone to live with you.'

'Bear didn't mean to run away,' his dad said firmly. 'That dog knows you love him, even if you said something you didn't mean. I'm guessing he jumped out that window to follow you, got himself scared in the car park, took off, and got lost. Wherever he is right now, he'll be wanting to get back to you.'

Lachlan tried to believe it, all through the next long day of looking and not finding, but it was getting harder to hope.

The day after that was going to be even worse.

It was the first day of school.

CHAPTER 11

Lachlan's new school was about a hundred and eighty-five times bigger than his old one. He felt as lost as Bear just following the receptionist down the halls to his classroom. He wondered if he'd ever find his way to the front gate again.

Although wandering around the halls would have been better than sitting in a class waiting for his turn to stand up and say who he was and the most exciting thing he'd done this summer. *'Hi, I'm Lachlan and what I did this summer was lose my dog.'*

Another boy, then a girl, then it would be his turn. The boy had just moved here too. He looked okay. The girl stood up.

'I'm Hannah, and the most exciting thing that happened to me this summer was last Friday my dad came home with a dog in the back of his ute. He must have jumped in but Dad doesn't know where. He's got shaggy black fur, a white neck, three white paws, and a really cute white stripe down his face. I call him Surprise, but—'

Lachlan jumped to his feet so fast his desk tipped over.

'His name is Bear!'

'Lachlan!' exclaimed the teacher.

'Sorry,' said Lachlan, and picked his desk up. 'But I lost my dog on Friday – and I think Hannah found him.'

The teacher decided that a lost-and-found dog was so exciting they could sort it out right then. Lachlan jumped to his feet again.

'Sit down, Lachlan,' the teacher said. 'You can't race off to the animal shelter in the middle of class. What you and Hannah can do is make sure all the facts add up.'

So they checked back and forth: 'And his ears point forward when he's listening—'

'And he loves to play ball!'

'But his name was on his tag!'

'We'd never heard of a dog named Bear – we thought it was your last name!'

The only thing they couldn't explain was how Bear had got into Hannah's dad's ute, because Terri's Takeaway where Lachlan had lost him wasn't anywhere near where Mr Cooper had been working.

And they still had to wait till after school to be absolutely positively one hundred per cent sure that it was really Bear in the Rainbow Street Shelter.

Their mums were waiting at the gate at the end of the day. The teacher had called them earlier.

'This is the girl who found Bear!' Lachlan shouted.

'This is the boy who lost Surprise!' shouted Hannah.

'We'll go straight there!' said Lachlan's mum.

'We'll show you the way,' said Hannah's mum.

Lachlan and his mum followed the other car through the streets towards the outskirts of town. They turned into 'Rainbow Street' and parked in front of the old house with the rainbow painted across the front and a three-legged goat grazing in the yard.

Lachlan could hardly breathe as they walked up the path and into the shelter. His mum put her hand on his shoulder, but when she spoke to Mona her voice was as shaky as Lachlan's hands.

'We think our dog is here.'

Hannah and Mrs Cooper stood at the shelter's back door and watched Lachlan and his mum cross to Surprise's run. But the dog wasn't Surprise anymore, he was Bear, and when he saw Lachlan he began to yip and howl as if he was telling him all about the terrible time he'd had. Mona opened the gate, and Bear threw himself against Lachlan, and Lachlan threw himself down to hug Bear as if they would never let each other go again.

Hannah went back inside. She was happy for Surprise, but she felt like crying.

'You could still change your mind about the guinea pig,' her mum said gently.

Hannah thought about the labrador Sam, and the frightened little dog with the five puppies, and all the other animals that needed to be comforted and played with while they waited for their owners or their new homes. She shook her head.

'I'll keep on coming,' she said.

'We'd better call your dad,' Lachlan's mum said, but her phone rang before she had time to open it. She listened for a moment and smiled. 'I think Lachlan would like to talk to you himself,' she said, handing the phone over.

'I've just talked to someone who was at a petrol station on Friday night,' said Dad, 'about ten kilometres up from where you lost Bear. He saw a border collie jump into the back of a ute.'

'It was my friend's dad's ute,' said Lachlan.

Lachlan, his mum and Bear walked back to the office. Hannah and her mum were still talking to Mona.

'Actually,' Mona was saying, 'the guinea pig

went to a new home yesterday. But if you're sure you still want to help, there are other dogs and cats who need the kind of care you gave Bear.'

'Can I help too?' asked Lachlan.

'We don't normally allow children—' Mona began.

'G'day, mate!' shrieked Gulliver, as Bert walked in.

'I give up,' said Mona. 'As long as you do exactly what Bert says, you can come too.'

That night, curled up snug on his bedroom floor with Bear, Lachlan talked to his dad again.

'Give him a hug for me,' said his dad. 'And one for you.'

'One for you too,' Lachlan said. He wiped his eyes with his sleeve.

Bear licked the phone.

Lachlan hugged him hard, just like his dad had asked.

CHAPTER 12

So, on Saturday mornings, and after school on Tuesdays, Hannah and Lachlan went to the Rainbow Street Shelter. Their mums took turns driving, and after the first week they stayed to help too. Lachlan's mum said that every time she helped a lost animal it was another thank you for finding Bear.

At first Mrs Cooper only wanted to help in the office, or wash things in the kitchen, but she always came out to see the dog that Hannah was feeding or playing with.

The black labrador Sam went home with a woman who lived near the beach.

'But I have another job for you,' said Bert. 'Those puppies will be old enough to go to new homes soon. We could start getting them used to kids.'

Hannah sat quietly in the run with the puppies. The mother dog watched her suspiciously, but finally decided that Hannah was not a danger, and even let her pat and pick up one fat squirmy puppy. He had a brown bottom, brown shoulders and a white middle: 'You look like a peanut!' Hannah whispered into his tiny white ear.

The next time she went, Bert and the mother dog let her take the puppies out to the playground. Hannah rolled on the ground with the puppies tumbling around her, but when the peanut puppy licked her face she stopped and sat under a tree to cuddle him against her. The puppy wriggled up and licked her face again with his pink tongue and milky breath; he scrambled over her legs and chewed on her finger with needle-sharp teeth. Hannah felt a warm balloon of love swell up inside her as she rolled the puppy on his back and tickled his fat tummy.

Lachlan was playing a tug-of-war with a bouncy Jack Russell. He waved to Hannah – and the dog yanked the toy out of his hand so that

Lachlan tumbled over backwards, the Jack Russell leaping proudly around him with the toy in his mouth.

Hannah felt a sharp stab of jealousy, because when Lachlan had cheered up the Jack Russell, he'd go home to Bear – but Hannah had to leave this puppy here.

She bent low over the puppy to hide her face, and the puppy caught her drooping ponytail. Hannah laughed, picked him up again – and saw something she'd never imagined could happen.

Her mother was in the run, squatting down to talk to the nervous little mother dog, patting and soothing her while Bert cleaned out the puppies' piddly papers.

Hannah and her mother were both very quiet in the car on the way home. Lachlan thought he knew why. He'd seen Hannah's face when she held the puppy, and even though he knew there'd never be another dog as special as Bear, he knew that Hannah could love that puppy just as much as he loved Bear.

'Do you want to come in and talk to Bear?' he asked, when they dropped him off.

Hannah shook her head no.

That night, Hannah heard her parents talking after she'd gone to bed. She couldn't hear what they were saying, but it sounded serious. She thought about how Lachlan and his mum had moved down here while his dad moved somewhere else, and all of a sudden she didn't feel jealous anymore.

The next day after school, Hannah's mum called her out to the front when her dad got home.

'Ready to go?' asked her dad.

'Where?' asked Hannah.

'Wait and see,' said her dad, but he was grinning and her mum was too.

They drove down the familiar roads and turned at Rainbow Street. 'But it's Friday!' said Hannah.

Her dad laughed when they walked into the shelter and Gulliver screeched, 'G'day, mate!' But Hannah didn't. All of a sudden, Hannah was hoping so badly she could hardly breathe, and she was trying not to hope it because she didn't think she could ever breathe again if it didn't come true this time.

Bert and Mona met them. They looked serious, but Bert winked at Hannah. They all walked out to the dog runs, straight across to the scruffy little mother dog and her puppies.

'Our fence isn't tall enough for a big dog like Bear,' said Hannah's dad. 'But it would be fine for a dog with shorter legs.'

'And the puppies aren't quite ready to go yet,' said Bert. 'There's time to fix up anything in your yard that needs fixing.'

Now Hannah couldn't speak or breathe. Her mother squeezed her hand. 'If you can come here to help these dogs, even though you thought they'd never be yours … we know you'll look after one of your own.'

'Is this the one?' Bert asked, scooping up the brown-and-white puppy and putting him in Hannah's arms.

'The only thing is …' said Hannah's mum, 'it probably won't be hard for the puppies to find good homes.'

Bert nodded.

Hannah held the puppy tighter.

'So what about the mother?' asked Hannah's mum.

'That'll be harder,' said Mona. 'She's not a very pretty dog.'

'She is so!' protested Hannah's mum. 'I was just worrying about how lonely she'll feel when all her puppies leave.'

'You think I should take the mother dog instead?' asked Hannah, and she knew she should feel happy to have any dog, but she belonged to this peanut puppy now and there was nothing she could do about it. The puppy squirmed closer to her face as if he thought so too.

'Of course not!' said her dad. 'Especially if the puppy's got anything to say about it.'

'The mother dog's for me,' said Hannah's mum.

Nelly and the
Dream Guinea Pig

CHAPTER 1

hen Nelly was a tiny, round brown-and-white puppy with short legs and a stumpy tail, she lived with a baby boy and his mother.

Nelly and the baby were together all the time. They rolled and tumbled across the floor and around the backyard. They played tug of war, splashed together in mud puddles, and dug in the sandpit.

When the baby cried, Nelly snuggled beside him till he felt better, fussing over him as if she were a mother dog and he was her puppy.

But when the baby was a nearly two-year-old walking, talking little boy, and Nelly was an already grown-up dog, the mother got a new job in a country on the other side of the world. She and her little boy had to move, and they couldn't take Nelly with them.

She asked all her family and friends, but no one had a place for Nelly. There was only one thing she could do: 'We'll take her to the Rainbow Street Shelter and ask them to find her a good home.'

Nelly walked happily under the painted rainbow and through the open door with the little boy and his mother.

'Can I help you?' squawked Gulliver.

Mona came into the waiting room. 'Gulliver likes being the receptionist,' she explained.

'Gulliver!' the cockatoo agreed in his croaky old-man's voice.

The little boy laughed.

But when his mother said goodbye to Nelly and lifted her into Mona's arms, he threw himself onto the floor, kicking and screaming in the loudest, most ferocious tantrum of his whole life. He did not want to leave without his friend.

With a wriggle and a squirm, Nelly leapt out

of Mona's arms. She snuggled in tight against the little boy's side, licking the tears off his face until he had to giggle.

Then his mother picked him up, Mona picked up Nelly, and they said goodbye. The mother felt like crying too, but she knew that this was the best place for the little stumpy-tailed dog to find a new home.

Mona met lots of dogs every day, but she had never met one who worked so hard at making someone feel better.

'Now you need someone to look after you!' she said when the boy and his mother had gone. She stroked firmly down Nelly's back, one hand after the other, over and over, till the bewildered dog was calm.

Bert came in the back door and smiled to see Mona sitting on the floor with the dog. He had never seen his busy friend look so relaxed.

'Will I take her out to a kennel now?' Bert asked gently.

'G'day, mate!' screeched Gulliver, flapping his wings at his friend.

'In a minute,' said Mona, still stroking Nelly.

But before she could get up, the door burst open and a man came in carrying a grey cat wrapped in a towel.

'He was running down the middle of the road, scared out of his wits!' the man said. 'I don't know where he came from.'

He put the cat-bundle down on the floor. Nelly leapt towards it. The cat hissed, spat and backed into a corner.

'Nelly!' shouted Mona.

'Sorry!' said the man.

'Can I help you?' screeched Gulliver.

'I think it's okay,' said Bert. 'Look.'

Nelly wasn't chasing the cat. Even when he waved a scratching claw at her nose, the little dog just crept forward on her belly, her head down and bottom up, stumpy tail wagging.

The grey cat stopped hissing.

Nelly crept closer and started to lick the frightened cat. The cat twitched his tail crossly but let the dog go on licking.

Finally, the cat gave himself a shake and jumped up onto the windowsill. He began smoothing his rumpled fur with neat grey paws, looking around the room as if he'd always been there.

'I've never seen anything like that!' said the man who'd rescued him.

'Neither have I,' said Bert.

'Nelly,' said Mona. 'I think you've found your home.'

So Nelly became Mona's dog and came to the shelter with her every day.

The grey cat stayed too. No one ever came to find him, and he never wanted to leave the office. Bert named him Minke, but even though Blanco loved Bert more than any other person, he never wanted to go home with him. He was happy just to curl up in his basket under the desk for the night.

Every morning Minke mewed and rushed to greet Nelly when she came in. Nelly licked his face till Minke blinked and leapt up to his windowsill to smooth her kisses off. For the rest of the day he sat there, watching everything that happened, letting people pat him if they asked politely, and keeping out of the way of the other dogs and cats as they came through the waiting room.

But Nelly liked meeting the people and animals that arrived feeling lost or worried. When puppies or kittens needed mothering, she stayed with them till they could be alone or were ready to be adopted. And if they were very young, Mona took them home at night so she could give them their midnight milk, and Nelly could snuggle them all night long.

CHAPTER 2

Samantha had always wanted a pet. All her life she'd thought she couldn't have one, because they lived in a flat high above the beach, and dogs and cats weren't allowed.

But on the second-last weekend of the school holidays, everything changed.

'What do you want to do for your birthday, Sam?' her mum asked, because Sam's birthday was next Sunday, and school went back the day after. Last year Sam had waited till school started to have a party, to make sure everyone could come.

'I don't need a party,' said Sam. 'I just want a pet.'

'WHAT?' her mother and father both said at

once, and so Sam said it again, because sometimes words didn't come out of her mouth the way they were supposed to, and she thought maybe she'd said something wrong.

In fact, Sam was so surprised herself at what had come out of her mouth this time that she nearly said 'WHAT?' too. She hadn't known she was going to ask for a pet – it was like a secret that her mind had been keeping even from her, and all of a sudden it had to burst out.

'I know I can't have a dog, or a cat,' she said quickly, before her parents could say it. 'But there are lots of other animals. Small animals that could live in a flat and don't have to go for walks.'

'What sort of animal?' asked her little brother, Liam.

'It would need a cage, whatever it is,' said her dad. 'You can't have something just running around the house.'

'It's still a whole week before my birthday,' said Sam. 'Couldn't we just go to the pet shop and see?'

Her parents looked at each other.

'Please?' she begged. 'I promise I won't ask to buy one today.'

'Is there even a pet shop around here?' her dad asked.

'No,' said her mum. 'But there's the animal shelter on Rainbow Street.'

Mr Ballart went to get the car keys.

Sam wasn't very good at dancing, but inside she was leaping like a rabbit in a brand new carrot patch.

The first animal they saw was a three-legged goat grazing on the lawn.

'Oh, the poor thing!' exclaimed Sam's mum.

'Can we take it home?' asked Liam.

'She'd eat the curtains,' said their dad.

Sam liked the way this goat didn't mind that it didn't have as many legs as other goats. She smiled at her as they went up the path.

They all went in the cherry-red door.

Gulliver and Mona both said at once, 'Can I help you?'

'We'd like to look at some small animals,' said Sam's mum.

'Just to get some ideas,' said her dad. 'We don't want to take a pet home today.'

Sam hardly heard them. A warm buzz of happiness was thrilling through her, because a little brown-and-white dog was sniffing her legs, a grey cat was grooming himself on the windowsill, and she knew that all around her were animals that needed someone to love. And one of them might be the right friend for her.

'No problem!' Gulliver screeched, in Mona's voice.

Maybe I could have a bird, thought Sam.

But Gulliver looked as if he belonged here, and he sounded as if he liked being the boss. Samantha felt a bit nervous around him. She wanted a little friend who needed to be patted and played with, and didn't tell her what to do.

'The rabbits are mostly outside,' said Mona, 'but the other ones you might like to see are in here.' She opened a door marked SMALL ANIMAL ROOM.

Liam stopped to talk to the little stumpy-tailed dog, but Sam and her mother and father followed Mona.

'Hi, everyone,' said Mona, looking around at the cages and hutches against the walls. 'You've got visitors.'

Mr and Mrs Ballart looked surprised.

'They don't understand exactly what I'm saying,' Mona admitted. 'But it seems only fair to tell them what's happening. Animals like being talked to, just like us.'

Sam hugged Mona's words inside herself. When she had her own pet, she would talk to it every day. She would tell it all her secrets, and her pet would never laugh if the words didn't come out right.

CHAPTER 3

Sam was almost glad she'd promised not to ask to take a pet home today.

There were so many animals in the room, and they were all so cute that she'd never have been able to decide. There were white rats, hooded rats, piebald mice and a mouse with a curly coat. There was a blonde guinea pig mother with three tiny golden babies.

'The babies won't be ready to leave their mum for another week,' said Mona.

Mona talked quietly to all the animals as she handled them. She showed Sam how to scoop up a mouse without squeezing its body, and put one of the piebald mice into Sam's cupped palm. The mouse's tiny body was warm in her hand.

'He's a bit skittish because he doesn't know you,' said Mona. 'So just hold his tail very gently, here right up against his body – don't ever hold a mouse by the tip of its tail, or you could break it off.'

'That's horrible!' said Sam, feeling sick.

'It would be,' Mona agreed. 'But holding it here doesn't hurt him, and it stops him jumping off your hand and hurting himself.'

When Sam put the mouse back, Mona gave her some sunflower seeds to feed a hooded rat, and showed her how to stroke the top of his head till he relaxed enough to climb into her hand. 'Now cover him with your other hand to stop him jumping off,' said Mona. 'But never hold his tail.'

Sam's head was whirling with trying to remember it all.

She patted the guinea pig mother, and held one of the babies in her hand, but the mother looked around so anxiously that Sam put the baby back before Mona asked her to.

They went back to the waiting room, where Liam was still sitting with the brown stumpy-tailed dog.

'I'm going to school soon,' he was telling Nelly. 'I'm a big boy now. I'm going to learn to read, and I'll have lots of friends and do EVERYTHING!'

Mona smiled at him. 'I see you've found a friend. Nelly loves everyone – animals and people – but I think she really misses having little kids in her life.'

Liam hugged the brown-and-white dog good-bye.

'You know,' Mona said gently, 'not all dogs are as friendly as Nelly. You shouldn't hug dogs you don't know.'

'Nelly,' said Liam, 'my name is Liam.' And he hugged her again.

Sam would have liked to hug Nelly too, but she wasn't sure if she should after what Mona had said, so she just patted her head.

'Go ahead,' said Mona. 'Nelly loves it. I just wanted your brother to understand that not all dogs are like that.'

Sam hugged Nelly, and the warmth of the dog's body melted away the muddle of wondering what animal she should choose.

As they left, Mona handed Sam some papers. 'These will tell you more about the different kinds of animals you met today and how to look after them. And you can come back any time and have another look. You'll know when you've found the animal that's right for you.'

Nelly stood at the door to watch the Ballarts leave.

'You liked that little boy, didn't you?' Mona asked, rubbing behind Nelly's ears. 'But they can't have a dog, and I couldn't do without you.'

Nelly leaned lovingly against Mona's legs. No matter how much she liked children, she and Mona belonged together, and she never wanted to leave.

CHAPTER 4

ow Sam had three things to be happy about. In one week it would be her birthday, and she'd go back to Rainbow Street to choose her pet. And the day after that, school would start.

Sam never told anyone that she was excited about going back to school. She knew what her friends would say. But Sam liked school.

She didn't like gym classes, since her arms and legs didn't always do exactly what she told them, and she didn't like the kids who teased her. What she liked was figuring out new things, like in her science extension classes – because Sam's brain was one part of her that worked just fine. Her best friends knew that, and they understood when words didn't come out the way she meant.

Still, Sam would have liked to be able to run fast along the beach, or jump high to catch a ball. When she watched Liam run and jump, she knew he was going to be happy at school right from the start. He wouldn't be laughed at or teased, because her little brother *could* run fast, jump high, and catch any ball, no matter who threw it.

Sam and her parents had read all the information sheets that Mona had given them, but they still couldn't decide which animal would be the best pet.

They learned that boy rats were usually cuddlier and girl rats were livelier, but that they could both learn to do tricks; that mice and rats needed toys to keep them busy, but that mice could get enough exercise by running in a wheel.

Mrs Ballart worried that rabbits needed too much room, and Mr Ballart worried that the fancy mice might escape.

Sam's mind was running in circles and getting nowhere, exactly like a mouse in its wheel.

'Don't worry,' said her mum, when she kissed her goodnight. 'It'll turn out okay.'

Sam tried to smile. She'd never thought it was going to be this hard to choose!

But that night, she dreamed of cuddling an animal with soft, thick hair. It was small but solid and sat quietly on her lap. It wasn't any of the animals that she'd actually held at the shelter.

'I want a guinea pig,' Sam said when she woke up.

She remembered the mother guinea pig with the little golden babies. *'They'll be ready to leave their mother in another week,'* Mona had said. That meant she could take one of the babies home on her birthday!

She would choose a girl baby, and she'd name it SugarSpice. The name just popped into her head, and Sam knew it was a sign that this was going to come true.

'Then the first thing to do,' said her dad when she told him, 'is to build a guinea pig cage.'

So straight after breakfast, Sam went to the computer and searched for a plan. She printed it out and then she and her dad went to the hardware store and bought everything they needed for SugarSpice's home.

They built the cage to fit into the hall between Sam and Liam's bedrooms, so it was longer than the one on the plan. It was a guinea pig palace.

It had a solid plastic bottom that would be easy to clean, and wire-grid sides so the guinea pig would be able to see everything going on in the hall around her, but couldn't climb out.

At one end there was a ramp up to the second storey. The second storey had a plastic floor and wire grid sides too, but it was only half as long as the bottom.

They put shredded paper on the floor, and finally they put in the wooden bedroom box, on the bottom floor so the guinea pig could find it easily. The box had one side open for a door, and a window cut out on each side. Sam imagined how she would peek in to see SugarSpice asleep in her bedroom.

When she tried to imagine holding SugarSpice, it didn't seem exactly like the solid little animal in her dream, but she knew that a baby guinea pig would grow and soon be just the way she pictured.

There were still five more days to wait.

'Could we go back and visit?' Sam asked her parents, but the weekend was over and they were busy.

'You know Mona said it was still a week before they could leave the mother,' said her mum.

'Just wait till your birthday,' said her dad. 'Your guinea pig will still be there.'

So Sam waited. She went to the library and found a book about looking after guinea pigs. She drew pictures for the walls of the cage and made up a guinea pig rhyme:

Guinea pig, guinea pig,
You're so nice.
That's why I call you
Sweet SugarSpice.

Sam's mum said that she could still have a party, so Sam wrote invitations to her three best friends to come to her house on Sunday afternoon for a 'Happy Birthday to Sam and welcome to Sugarspice' party.

The night before her birthday, she dreamed her guinea pig dream again. SugarSpice was all grown up, and her fur had turned from golden to black. *Dreams are strange!* Sam thought.

But the strongest thing in the dream was the warm honey feeling of happiness, just sitting and stroking her animal friend. That was the part she knew was true.

So right after breakfast, when Sam had opened the guinea pig card Liam had drawn her and the guinea pig book that her parents had bought, the whole family went to the Rainbow Street Shelter.

'Can I help you?' shrieked the cockatoo.

Liam threw his arms around Nelly and started telling her all about getting ready to go to school tomorrow.

Mona came out of the SMALL ANIMAL ROOM, and Sam rushed in.

The hutch with the blonde guinea pig mother and her three babies was empty.

SugarSpice wasn't there.

CHAPTER 5

'Someone wanted the mother as well as the babies, so we didn't have to wait,' Mona was saying to Sam's parents. 'Guinea pigs are always happier when they've got company, even when they're grown-up.'

Mr and Mrs Ballart looked at each other sadly. They knew how upset Sam was going to be if she couldn't have the baby guinea pig.

But Sam was too amazed to be upset – because there, in another hutch in the corner, was the guinea pig from her dream.

He was fat, black and whiskery. Sam squatted down beside him. 'Hello, Henry,' she said.

'Are you sure?' asked her mother. 'I thought you wanted a baby one.'

'A pet has to be the right one for you,' said Mona.

'He's the absolutely perfect one,' said Sam.

Mona smiled, and put Henry into Sam's waiting hands. He felt exactly like he had in the dream: soft, warm and solid. His black hair was spiky and his whiskers stuck out, but he was the cutest guinea pig Sam had ever seen.

He was so cute that Sam was suddenly sure there was a mistake and that he already belonged to someone else.

'Does he need a home?' she asked. The words came out fine, but her voice was quivery.

'I think he's just found one,' said Mona.

Sam's birthday-and-welcome-Henry party wasn't big, but it was the best party she'd ever had.

She carried Henry around so he could see every room in the flat. She introduced him to her friends and let them pat him. But Mona had said to let him have some time to get used to his new home, so after everyone had said hello, Sam put him into the guinea pig palace.

Henry scurried around his shredded paper bedding. He had a drink from his water bottle and ate some pellets. Then he went into his wooden bedroom box. Sam peeked through the little window, but she couldn't tell if he was asleep or just resting. He was very quiet.

But when Sam's friends had gone home, and her parents were in the kitchen and Liam had gone to bed, Henry came out.

'Hi there, Henry,' said Sam. 'Are you hungry?'

She held out a piece of celery. Henry came closer. He was still shy, but he wanted that celery.

Finally he came close enough to nibble the end. 'Yum, yum, celery!' said Sam, still holding it. She didn't mind what she said to Henry because she knew he would know what she meant, and know that she was his friend.

Henry's cheeks puffed, his nose wiggled, and his teeth crunched as fast as they could. The celery disappeared right up to the last bit in Sam's fingers.

'Do you want some carrot now?' Sam asked, and went to the kitchen to get it.

When she came back, Henry was not being

quiet at all. He was exploring his cage, chirping and whistling, scurrying up the ramp to the top floor and down again.

Henry was a very happy guinea pig.

Maybe Mona was wrong, Sam thought. Maybe most guinea pigs liked to have other guinea pigs for company – but Henry just needed Sam.

All the rest of that day Nelly had wagged her stumpy tail at the people and pets who came in. She'd gone out to the runs in the back to sniff noses with the dogs that were waiting to find homes. She'd let a lost border collie bounce all around her until he felt calm again – but Mona knew that something wasn't quite right.

'How about we go to the beach on our way home?' Mona said, and Nelly pricked up her ears.

Nelly liked the beach. It had soft sand to dig and shallow waves to run in – but best of all, it had children. Kids who talked to her, kids who threw her a ball, kids who stroked her head and rubbed her freckled pink tummy when she rolled onto her back.

She led Mona past one group of kids after another, collecting pats until her round brown eyes were glowing with happiness.

'Oh, Nelly,' sighed Mona as the little dog settled happily onto the back seat on the way home. 'I'm sorry I don't know any kids for you to visit.'

CHAPTER 6

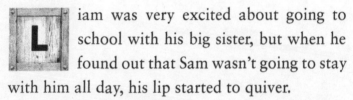

Liam was very excited about going to school with his big sister, but when he found out that Sam wasn't going to stay with him all day, his lip started to quiver.

'You'll make lots of friends!' said their mum, and hugged him again as Sam waved goodbye.

Sam was excited too. She knew her words would come out just right when it was her turn to stand up and tell the class: 'The best thing I did this summer was get a guinea pig from the Rainbow Street Shelter.'

It was nearly her turn when Hannah stood up and said, 'Last Friday my dad came home with a dog in the back of his ute ... He's got shaggy black fur, a white neck, three white paws, and a really cute stripe down his face.'

That sounds like a dog I saw at the shelter! Sam thought, just as Lachlan shouted, 'His name is Bear!'

By the time they'd sorted out that Hannah's Surprise was really Lachlan's Bear, Sam knew her story didn't sound very dramatic.

But when she told it, the teacher said, 'It sounds like Rainbow Street was a busy place last weekend: lost-and-found dogs, and adopted guinea pigs!'

Hannah turned around and smiled at Sam, her ponytail swinging. 'I'm glad!' she whispered.

'So am I!' Sam whispered back.

Liam's day hadn't been nearly as good.

'Didn't you make any friends?' Sam asked.

Liam shook his head. 'There are too many kids! I don't want to talk to so many kids!'

'You'll get used to it,' said Sam. She wanted her little brother to be happy and brave at school right from the start.

That night, Liam showed his reader to his mum and told her the story. He could already read a

85

few words because of the books his parents and Sam read to him at home.

'Your teacher's going to be very pleased with you!' said their mum.

'There are too many kids!' Liam said again. 'I'm not going to do it at school!'

Sam was suddenly so angry she thought she was going to burst. Liam could talk so well and do everything so easily – it wasn't fair if he didn't even bother!

She marched to her bedroom. She would have gone in and slammed the door with a bang, if Henry's cage hadn't been in the hall beside it.

She took the guinea pig out of his cage and carried him to her room. Henry sat quietly on her lap, just like he had in her dream. She held him up to her shoulder so his furry head tickled her neck.

It's hard to be mad when you're holding a fat, furry guinea pig.

And it's hard not to laugh when that fat, furry guinea pig tickles your neck.

Sam went to get an apple from the fridge, shutting her bedroom door behind her. When she came back Henry had disappeared.

'Henry!' Sam called softly. 'Henry, where are you?' She wasn't sure if he was supposed to be loose in her bedroom, and she didn't want her mum to know that she couldn't find him.

After a moment she heard a rustling under her bed. Sam lay down on the floor and looked into a pair of bright eyes.

'Hey there,' she whispered.

Henry stared back.

Sam rolled the red apple over to the bed. Henry came closer. Sam pushed it gently towards him till the apple was nearly touching the guinea pig's nose.

Henry crept forward. He tried to bite the apple, and the apple rolled back out from under the bed. Nudge by nudge and nibble by nibble, Henry rolled the apple to the middle of the room. Sam sat quietly and watched him. When the apple rolled towards her she pushed it gently back.

By the time her mum called her for dinner, the apple had rolled back and forth and around the room five times. Now it was resting against her desk and Henry was nibbling white chunks out of its red skin. Sam moved slowly towards him, and picked him up.

'Thank you, Henry,' she whispered, because she'd been a bit worried she mightn't have been able to catch him. She snuggled him close for a second, and put him back in his cage.

'Samantha!' her mother called again.

Sam got a tissue and quickly picked up a few little black pellets from the floor. She flushed them down the toilet, washed her hands, and raced to the kitchen.

Her mum was already sitting at the table, but Sam threw her arms around her and hugged her tight. 'Henry's the best present I ever got,' she said.

'I'm glad,' said her dad, and Sam hugged him too.

'I love Henry,' said Liam, and Sam couldn't be cross at him anymore.

She brought Henry out of his cage again after dinner and let Liam hold him.

CHAPTER 7

Sometimes Sam wished she could let Liam take Henry to school, because holding the guinea pig made her feel good, no matter what else was wrong, and she knew he made Liam happy too. But even if guinea pigs were allowed to go to school, Henry wouldn't like being in the middle of a bunch of noisy kids any more than Liam did.

On Friday evening the Ballart family went to the beach. Sam almost didn't want to go, because she'd been away from Henry all day at school, and it seemed mean to leave him alone again now.

'Come on, Sam!' called her dad. 'You can't stay home on your own!'

'Give Henry a bit of fresh hay and he'll be fine!' said her mum.

The guinea pig's whiskery black face stared at her. She knew he was saying, '*It's time for me to have a play outside the cage!*'

'We'll have the apple game when I get back,' Sam promised.

It was so hot that even Mr Ballart went for a swim. Liam splashed and their mum swam back and forth between the flags, but Sam stayed in the water the longest, jumping over the little waves and catching the bigger ones on her boogie board until she was shivery and tired.

Liam was already wrapped in his towel when she came out.

'Look!' he shouted suddenly.

Mona and Nelly were splashing along the water's edge.

Liam raced across the sand and threw his arms around the little brown-and-white dog. Nelly licked his face. Mr and Mrs Ballart came over to get Liam, and Mona laughed.

'How's the guinea pig?' she asked Sam.

'He whistles a lot,' said Sam, 'and he jumps around his cage.'

'Then he's happy,' said Mona.

Sam felt so warm inside she stopped shivering under her towel. If Mona said he was happy, Sam didn't have to feel guilty that he didn't have a guinea pig friend.

'I can read, too!' Liam was telling Nelly. 'Do you want me to tell you the story?'

The little dog snuggled against him as if she was saying yes, and Liam told her the story from his latest reader.

'Why doesn't he do that at school?' Sam asked her dad. 'It's so easy for him!'

'It doesn't matter how good people are at things,' said her dad, 'they still have to get up the nerve to do them. Not everyone's as brave as you.'

Sam knew he was joking, because she wasn't brave at all. She just did what she wanted to do, even things that were hard for her, because that was better than not doing them at all.

'That's what brave means,' whispered her dad, as if he knew what she was thinking.

Liam was still talking to Nelly. 'Time to go

home,' his mum said gently, but the little round dog rolled on her back, waving her paws for Liam to rub her speckly pink tummy.

'Nelly does love talking to kids!' Mona laughed. 'I bet she wishes she could go to school with you!'

Everyone laughed, but at the back of Sam's mind, an idea started to grow.

Early Saturday morning, a young man turned up at the Rainbow Street Shelter holding a small tan-and-white guinea pig.

'I found this under a bush when I took my dog out for a run!' he said. 'It was lucky the dog was on a leash, because she saw it before I did.'

Nelly trotted out from behind the desk and sniffed the man's legs, looking up at the animal he was holding. The man held the guinea pig higher.

'It's okay,' said Mona. 'Nelly welcomes all the animals. They seem to know she wants to help them.'

The man looked surprised, but held the guinea pig lower so Nelly could sniff it. The guinea pig wiggled out of his hands to the floor.

'Oh, no!' shouted the man.

'No problem!' screeched Gulliver.

The grey cat on the windowsill stopped halfway through combing the top of his head with his paws.

Mona shut the door. 'It's okay,' she said again, because Nelly had curled herself around the guinea pig, nuzzling and licking it till the frightened animal stopped quivering.

'Have you got any idea where he might have escaped from?' Mona asked.

The man shook his head. 'I asked everyone I saw. They all thought I was joking when I asked if they'd lost a guinea pig!'

'They can go further than you'd think, once they get loose,' Mona said. 'Now we just have to hope his owners think of looking for him here!'

'What happens if they don't?' asked the man.

'I'm sure we'll be able to find him a new home,' said Mona. 'But we'll wait for a week to give his owners a chance to find him first.'

'Good luck, Piggie!' said the man, and left.

Mona filled a small water dish and put it in front of the guinea pig. Then she got a cage ready, with clean hay and a little house for the guinea pig to hide in when he wanted.

'You can't stay out here in the waiting room,' she told him as she picked him up. 'You never know what big dog or cat might come in – and they're not all as nice as Nelly!'

She checked him over. He wasn't a baby, but he wasn't quite grown up yet.

'Poor lost little boy!' Mona murmured. 'You're a bit thin, too – I think you might have been loose for a while.' But she couldn't find any cuts or sores; his eyes and ears looked healthy and so did his teeth. 'I think you'll be okay when you stop being so scared.' Mona placed him gently in the cage in the SMALL ANIMAL ROOM.

Nelly curled up beside it. The guinea pig stayed right where Mona had put him, just inside the cage door.

'Okay,' said Mona. 'If that's what you both want!'

She opened the cage again, and the little guinea pig nestled up to Nelly as if he was going home to his mother.

CHAPTER 8

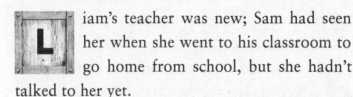iam's teacher was new; Sam had seen her when she went to his classroom to go home from school, but she hadn't talked to her yet.

Sam always worried more about her words coming out wrong when she talked to someone for the first time. Especially when she was going to tell them a crazy idea.

But maybe she wouldn't need to. Maybe Liam would be so happy this week that Sam could drop her crazy idea before she even had to explain it to anyone.

The teacher smiled at her when she went to meet Liam on Monday afternoon.

'My brother's getting good at reading, isn't he?' Sam said.

She was hoping the teacher would say, '*Yes, he is!*' or '*You must have given him lots of help for him to read so well already!*'

But the teacher said, 'Don't worry. Lots of the kids are too shy to read out loud at the start of the year. It just takes them a while to warm up.'

'He's not so shy when he talks to dogs,' said Sam.

The teacher laughed, as if Sam was joking. 'I'll remember that if I find a dog in my classroom one day!'

Sam decided she'd tell Mona her idea before she talked to the teacher – and first of all, she had to ask her parents.

She waited till Liam had gone to bed, and it was just her, alone with her mum and dad, then she told them her idea. 'I know it sounds crazy,' she said, 'but you know how much Liam loves telling Nelly stories!'

'But...' said her mother.

'The teacher said lots of the kids are shy,' Sam rushed on, before her mum could think exactly what the 'But' was going to be. 'So it would help all of them, not just Liam.'

'Why do you want to do this so badly?' asked her dad.

Sam didn't know how to answer. Liam was her little brother and she wanted him to be happy at school – but she didn't know exactly why it was so important that he should do well at the things she knew he could do.

'School wasn't very easy for you at the start, was it, Sam?' asked her mum.

Sam shook her head. 'No.'

'You never told us,' said her dad, 'but we knew.'

'I'd just like it to be nicer for Liam,' said Sam.

'We'd have liked it to be nicer for you,' said her dad.

'It's good now,' said Sam.

'Okay,' said her mum. 'We'll go to see Mona tomorrow when I pick you up after school.'

Mona was surprised when Mrs Ballart, Sam and Liam turned up at Rainbow Street again the next day. Liam rushed to Nelly and threw himself down on the floor beside her.

'Is there a problem with Henry?' Mona asked.

'Henry's fine,' said Sam. 'Except he's probably a bit cross because I haven't let him out of his cage yet this afternoon.'

Mona smiled. 'We've got one now who got out of his cage and into the big wide world! Luckily someone found him and brought him in here. He's been eating all weekend, and he's already not quite so thin. He's not so nervous, either, and Nelly doesn't think he needs her there all the time anymore. This morning she just stayed with him for an hour or so, before she came back to the waiting room. But unfortunately nobody's phoned about a runaway guinea pig.'

She showed Sam the little tan-and-white guinea pig. He was much smaller than Henry, and he still looked lost and lonely. Sam patted him while she waited for her mum to tell Mona why they were there.

'Tell Mona your idea, Sam,' said Mum.

Liam had opened his school bag and was showing his reader to Nelly. It was the perfect way to explain what she meant. Sam took a deep breath.

'I wondered if Nelly could be a reader dog,' she said.

'Sorry, but no!' said Mona.

Sam felt her brilliant idea shrivel and die.

'Nelly's not for adoption,' Mona went on. 'She's mine, and the shelter's. She belongs here.'

'I didn't mean to adopt!' Sam protested, imagining how she'd feel if someone wanted to take Henry away. 'I just wondered if you'd like to bring Nelly to visit Liam's class so they could read to her.'

'And that's the end of the story,' Liam said to Nelly, and closed his book. Nelly licked him and rolled on her back.

Mona smiled. 'Sam, that's a really wonderful idea,' she said.

All the next morning, no matter what Sam's teacher was saying in class, Sam was wondering what Liam's teacher would say that afternoon.

She might think Sam was crazy. She might laugh. She might hate dogs – or just say that it was against the rules.

At lunchtime, Hannah told Sam about the puppies at the Rainbow Street Animal Shelter. 'After school I'm taking them into the playground, so they get used to playing with kids.'

'That sounds so fun!'

'How's your guinea pig?' Hannah asked, as if she'd suddenly remembered that dogs weren't the only pets in the world.

'He whistles when I come into the room,' said Sam. 'You can come and see him sometime if you want.' And then Sam told Hannah her idea.

'How did you come up with such an amazing plan?' said Hannah.

'The teacher mightn't think it is,' Sam pointed out.

'Well, at first Mona and my parents thought I was too young to be a volunteer at the shelter,' Hannah said. 'But Bert said he was probably too old, and if you added our ages up we were both just right. So everybody gave in.'

Sam laughed. Still, she wished she could be as brave as Hannah when she went to see Liam's teacher.

'A reading dog?' repeated Liam's teacher when Sam told her. 'What a fantastic idea!'

Sam beamed. She'd never thought it would be this easy!

'Of course it's not up to me,' the teacher added. 'You'll have to talk to the principal. It's too bad she's allergic to dogs.'

Sam didn't want to go to see the principal one little bit. She was wishing she'd never thought of this stupid idea. Why did it even matter if her little brother wasn't brave when he'd just started school?

'Do you want me to go with you?' her mum asked.

Maybe the whole idea won't sound nearly so crazy if Mum explains it, Sam thought. But she said, 'No, thanks. I'll do it myself.'

So she started getting ready.

She looked up 'reading dogs' online, and found out that maybe her idea wasn't so crazy after all. She printed out three articles, and made a poster with a picture her mum had taken of

Liam and Nelly. Across the top she wrote in great big letters:

NELLY: THE READING DOG FOR OUR SCHOOL!

Then she lay on the rug in her bedroom, watching Henry roll a cardboard tube across the floor. She didn't know if he was trying to roll it or if he was trying to chew it and it was rolling away. It didn't matter: he was having fun, and she was having fun watching him.

And the longer she watched him, and especially when she held him against her cheek before putting him back in his cage for the night, the happier she felt. Suddenly a little voice in her head said that maybe there was a simpler way to make Liam happier and braver.

Sam didn't want to listen to that little voice. Liam could do lots of things; having a guinea pig was a special thing that was just hers. She didn't want to share it.

CHAPTER 9

I t was a busy morning at the Rainbow Street Shelter. Mona unlocked the front door with one hand and answered her phone with the other.

'I can hear a kitten mewing in the garden,' said an anxious woman, before Mona could even say hello. 'But I can't find it – and I've got to leave for work soon.'

'I'll be there as soon as I can,' said Mona, opening the door. Minke was stepping out of his basket under the desk, meowing and stretching. Nelly rushed in to greet him, then into the SMALL ANIMAL ROOM to check her guinea pig, and finally into the hospital room to see a dog who'd come in with a broken leg the day before.

'Can I help you?' Gulliver was screeching from his perch above the desk.

Mona checked the hospital animals and gave the dog a needle to stop the broken leg from hurting. Nelly licked the dog's face while Mona gave him the injection.

'G'day, mate!' Gulliver shrieked, and Bert came in.

'I think Nelly helps as much as the medicine!' he said, rubbing the little dog's head.

'I'll take her with me now,' said Mona. 'I have to go and find a lost kitten.'

Mona drove out to the woman's house and Nelly helped her search the garden. It didn't take her long to find five tiny kittens. They were so new their eyes were still shut, and they were chilly and weak. Nelly started licking them right away – she knew that if they didn't get warm soon they could die.

'You're right, Nelly,' said Mona, as she nestled the kittens into a soft towel in the bottom of a cat-carry cage. 'I don't know what happened to their mum, but these babies are really missing her!'

'What if the mother comes back?' asked the woman who'd phoned.

'Call us right away,' said Mona. 'But it looks as though they've been on their own for a while. The most important thing now is to get some milk into them.'

The woman touched one of the tiny heads with her finger. 'I really don't want a cat,' she said, but she didn't sound very sure, and when she rushed away to work she had tears in her eyes.

'Wouldn't surprise me if you see her again when you're bigger,' Mona told the kittens, and put the carry cage gently into the back of her car.

When they got back to the shelter, Bert and Mona fed the kittens with a special kitty bottle, and then put them into a box where Nelly licked them clean. The abandoned kittens nestled up against her, purring gently.

At lunchtime, when everyone else was going out to play, Sam went to see the principal. Her stomach was a tight knot and she was afraid her tongue might be too. Her hand didn't want to knock on the office door.

But somehow it did, and when Mrs Stevens told her to come in, her legs did what they were told – and then there was nothing she could do but explain her idea.

'You know how some little kids don't like reading out loud because they think people are going to laugh at them?'

Mrs Stevens nodded.

'If they read to a dog they might get braver, because dogs never laugh at you.'

'That's true,' said Mrs Stevens.

Sam held up her reading dog poster.

'I know a dog who's so gentle that she even looks after sick animals – and she *loves* little kids! And Mona said she could bring her here once a week to visit Liam's class.'

'That's a very good idea!' said Mrs Stevens.

Sam took a deep breath. She'd been ready to explain all about the shelter, and now she didn't know what to do with all those words crowding to get out.

'I thought you were allergic!' she said instead. And then she turned red, because that didn't sound like the sort of thing you were supposed to say to a principal.

'I am,' said Mrs Stevens. 'And some kids may be too. There'll be lots of details to sort out – but it's a great idea, and I think we should try.'

CHAPTER 10

o Mona took Nelly to Liam's class for the first visit on Friday afternoon – and Sam was invited too.

A special corner was set up with a comfy mat for Nelly. The children took turns going up to the mat with their book and sitting down beside her. Sam and Mona sat in chairs behind the mat, close enough that Mona was there for Nelly, but not so close that they seemed to be listening to the story.

Liam went first. He showed Nelly his reader, pointing out the pictures and making up the story when he didn't know the words. He read so clearly that Mona and Sam could hear every word, and his teacher smiled in surprise.

When the story was finished, Nelly rolled on her back and let him rub her pink freckled tummy for a minute – and then it was someone else's turn.

Nelly listened to every child as if she couldn't believe how lucky she was, and as if this was the best story she'd ever heard. She didn't laugh when they said words wrong, and she didn't correct them when they didn't know what the words were. She just let them tell the story the way they wanted.

A few kids didn't even try to read, but they whispered secrets to her, and Nelly wagged their sadness away.

Sam watched the kids get happier and braver as they sat with the little dog. She saw how they stood up taller when they went back to their desks after rubbing Nelly's tummy. She started to feel as warm and happy as when she cuddled Henry, and from the way Mona was smiling too, Sam knew that she was feeling exactly the same way.

The teacher asked the children to thank Mona and Nelly as they left.

'And let's thank Samantha for organising it,' she added.

Liam jumped up and hugged his sister. All the other children followed, jumping around Sam in a giant group hug that nearly knocked her over.

'Thank you!' they squealed.

Even though Sam had talked about other kids when she'd told the teachers her plan, she'd really only been thinking about her own little brother. She'd never thought all the others were going to be just as happy as Liam. She hadn't known it would make her feel so good.

It was their dad's turn to pick them up from school.

'I think we should celebrate Sam's great idea!' he said. 'I've got your bathers and towels...how about we go straight to the beach, and then meet your mum for dinner?'

Their mum's office was in a tall building in town. They walked around the corner to a restaurant with candles on the tables. Sam had spaghetti, and fruit salad with ice-cream for dessert.

'This is one of the best days of my life!' said Sam.

'Me too!' said Liam.

It was late when they went home. Liam fell sound asleep in the car and Sam nearly did. She was ready to tumble into her bed. But as she walked down the hall to her bedroom, there was a rustling and whistling. Henry was standing up against the side of his cage, waiting for his playtime and treats.

'Oh, Henry!' said Sam. 'I forgot all about you!'

She picked him up and cuddled him against her chin. Henry wiggled – he wanted to get down on the floor and run around.

'Hop straight into bed, Sam!' called her mum.

'But Henry's lonely!' Sam protested.

'You can talk to him in the morning,' said her mum.

So Sam snuck in a piece of celery for Henry to eat in his cage, and went to bed. She couldn't believe she'd forgotten about her little friend.

CHAPTER 11

'I've been thinking,' said Sam the next morning. 'It's not fair for Henry to be all alone in his cage when I don't come home to play with him.'

'You can't stay home all the time to look after a guinea pig!' said her dad.

'That's not what I mean ...' said Sam.

Sam took an apple back to her room while she waited for her parents to talk about her idea. She let Henry roll it from one side of the room to the other. She opened up a big brown paper bag for him to crawl inside and explore.

'I'll never let you be lonely again!' she whispered.

'Sam!' her dad called.

Sam picked Henry up. The guinea pig was happy now he'd had his play, and whuffled quietly under Sam's chin as she went back to the kitchen.

'You sure about this?' her dad asked.

'I'm sure,' said Sam.

'Look, Nelly!' Mona called as the Ballarts came in the cherry-red door. 'Here are some of your favourite people!'

Nelly trotted out from where she'd been snuggling with the kittens and rushed to Liam.

'She's been really happy since we visited the school,' Mona told Sam. 'And how's Henry?'

'He's lonely,' said Sam.

'I think I know what you're thinking,' said Mona. 'Nelly!' she called. 'We're going to say hello to your piggie friend.'

Nelly led them into the SMALL ANIMAL ROOM, where the little tan-and-white guinea pig was sitting in his hutch.

'He hasn't been claimed, so he's ready to go to

a new home today,' Mona said. She opened the door and picked up the guinea pig. 'He's young, so he and Henry should get along. But you still have to be sure you can love him too.'

She put him into Sam's arms.

'He's not for me,' said Sam. And she gave the guinea pig to her brother.

Liam's eyes opened wide with surprise. He was too excited to speak as the guinea pig scrambled up against his chest.

Nelly licked them both until the guinea pig and the boy knew she'd made them belong together.

'What's his name?' Liam asked at last.

'He's waiting for you to tell him,' said Mona.

'Gingersnap,' said Liam.

When they got home, they put a beach towel on the living-room floor. Sam sat at one end with Henry, and Liam sat at the other end with Gingersnap. After a while they each put their guinea pigs down.

Gingersnap stayed close to Liam. Henry started to explore the new room, and then stopped and sniffed. He could smell a new guinea pig, and he was deciding whether it was a friend or an enemy.

Henry stomped towards Gingersnap. His hackles were up to make him look bigger, and he held his nose high in the air.

Gingersnap quivered so he looked even smaller. He put his nose down low.

Henry sniffed him all over – then scampered off across the floor, looking behind him as if asking his new friend if he wanted to come too. Gingersnap started to follow, though when Henry turned around, he bolted back to hide behind Liam's legs.

When it was time to put them both into the guinea pig palace between Sam and Liam's rooms, Henry flipped and scampered for joy, up and down the ramp and all over the cage.

After a little while, Gingersnap did too.

Mona and the
Lion Cub

CHAPTER 1

For as long as she could remember, Mona had loved animals. Some of her friends loved dogs, some loved cats, and others were crazy about rabbits, but Mona loved all animals.

Her mother said that when Mona was a baby, she'd learned to walk by holding onto her grandparents' dog. The dog was a golden retriever, strong but gentle, and he'd let baby Mona grab his curly blond fur to pull herself up.

Maybe that was why Mona had always known that when she grew up, she was going to work with animals. But somehow, when she did grow up, she thought that working with animals wasn't a proper grown-up job, and she went to work in an office. She worked hard and earned money, but she wasn't really happy.

Then, one day Mona went back to the house where her grandparents had lived when she was a little girl. It looked as if no one had loved it for a long time. The paint was peeling off and one front window was broken.

It wasn't the busy, happy home Mona remembered. She was glad her grandparents couldn't see it now.

As she stood with her hand on the gate, almost wishing she didn't have to go in, a three-legged goat trotted out from behind a tree.

Mona stared in surprise. 'Hi there!' she called, and walked up the path.

CHAPTER 2

n a trailer at the back of a circus, a lioness rustled her straw into a soft bed. Her sister lioness and the roaring, shaggy-maned lion were performing in the circus Big Top. Right this minute the crowd was gasping as they leapt through fiery hoops.

This lioness was resting. She was tired and her belly was huge. She was getting ready to have cubs.

The summer Mona turned eight was the most magical summer of her whole life.

Her family was going to visit her grandparents,

right on the other side of the country. But for the first time ever, Mona was going to stay for the whole summer while her mum and dad went back to their busy jobs in the city. She was a little bit scared, and very, very excited.

Gran and Grandpa McNeil lived on the edge of a town near the beach, in a small blue house on Rainbow Street.

'We saw a rainbow the very first time we came here,' Gran explained. 'Our house was right under the middle of the arch.'

'We knew it would be a place where dreams could come true,' said Grandpa.

Mona's dream was that this year her parents would let her have a pet of her own for Christmas.

'You'll have all the pets you want, all summer,' her mum said.

'But I want to bring one home,' said Mona.

'Our lives are just too busy for a pet,' said her dad.

Gran and Grandpa sometimes said they were too busy to have any more pets too – but the next time they heard about a stray that needed a home, they always said it could come and live with them till it found somewhere better. Somehow, the animals never found anywhere better.

That's why they had five dogs. They had Goldie, the very old dog who'd taught Mona to walk. Next was Freckles, a little speckly dog who'd just followed Grandpa home one day. Then two little sausage dogs, Frieda and Vicky, needed a home when the old lady who owned them went to hospital. Buck was a sort-of-border collie, with a white face and a black patch over one eye; he'd turned up in a thunderstorm and they never found out where he came from.

When Mona and her parents had visited the year before, Gran and Grandpa had a brand-new baby goat named Heidi. Heidi was a twin, but she was smaller and weaker than her brother, and the mother goat didn't have enough milk to feed both of them. 'This little one will die if someone doesn't look after it,' Heidi's owner said. 'But I'm too busy to give her a bottle every two hours!'

Gran didn't care about being too busy when there was a baby animal to save. She'd taken the tiny white kid and fed her special goat milk from a baby bottle. She'd put old towels in a box in the kitchen and tucked the baby goat into it.

Mona had loved the way Heidi snuggled against her, hungrily sucking her fingers. She'd loved feeding her the bottle, even though the kid sometimes nudged her so hard that the milk had spurted all over both of them. And she'd loved taking the tiny goat out to the garden to run and play.

Sometimes in the evenings, if Grandpa fell asleep on the couch, Heidi had climbed on top of him and curled up to sleep on his chest.

But now Heidi was nearly grown-up. She lived outside, and played tag games with Buck the collie. All the McNeils' animals lived happily together, even the ones who could have been enemies.

When the circus was asleep, four tiny cubs were born in the trailer behind the tents. The mother lioness licked them clean and snuggled around them in the straw bed. Three of the cubs began to nurse, but the last one born, the tiniest of all, was too sleepy to try.

CHAPTER 3

I t was such a long way to Gran and Grandpa's house that Mona's mum and dad couldn't come back again for Christmas.

'So we're having Christmas tomorrow!' said Gran on the night they arrived.

Mona was already so excited it was easy to believe. And it was easy to wake up Christmas-morning early, because the time was three hours earlier at Rainbow Street than it was at home. At first she was sad that she'd left the presents for her mum and dad behind, but when she peeked under the tree, she saw her mum had brought them.

124

'But we have to wait for Uncle Matthew,' said Grandpa, hugging her good morning.

Uncle Matthew was Mona's dad's younger brother. Except for their red hair and bright-blue eyes, they were as different as two brothers could be. Mona's father worked in an office and was always worried, but Uncle Matthew was a juggler in a circus, and never worried about anything.

The circus travelled all over the country. Mona and her parents had seen it in their city the winter before. They'd watched Uncle Matthew juggle small bright balls and long striped batons. And when all the lights went off, Mona knew that the person in the middle of the ring, tossing flaming torches high into the blackness, was her very own Uncle Matthew.

His circus was coming to town today.

So, late that afternoon, when everything was set up and ready for the show the next day, Uncle Matthew came to Rainbow Street. Now it really felt like Christmas. They had barbecued prawns and fancy salads, and Christmas pudding with ice-cream and custard... and then finally, they had the presents.

Mona's parents gave her a Barbie doll in a pink bathing suit, and Gran and Grandpa gave her the book *Charlotte's Web*, about a runty pig and the spider that saved its life. Uncle Matthew's present was an envelope. Inside it were three tickets to the circus, and a note:

```
Merry Early Christmas!

These tickets include a Behind-the-Scenes
Tour to see Amazing, Fearsome and Cute
Animals with your favourite uncle.
```

Early the next morning, Mona's mother and father took a taxi back to the airport. Mona wouldn't see them again till the end of the holidays. For a minute it was a very lonely feeling. Gran held her hand as she waved goodbye.

Then Buck nosed her a ball to throw, and Grandpa said, 'Four more hours till the circus!'

It was the best circus Mona had ever seen. The clowns tumbled and tripped, while poodles in jackets balanced on rolling barrels. A lioness jumped through a hoop as the lion-trainer cracked his whip. The huge lion watched from his stool and roared, his tail swishing angrily. Mona and her grandparents were sitting so close they could see his pink tongue and sharp pointed teeth.

Then Uncle Matthew was dancing on tall stilts and juggling silvery rings. Mona clapped till her hands were sore. She held her breath when the tightrope-walker teetered wildly on the high-wire, and imagined the feeling of flying when the spangled girl-acrobat soared free from one swing to another. But all the while she was wondering what she was going to see after the show.

Finally, after the grand parade, when the rest of the audience was going home, full to the brim with amazement and popcorn, Uncle Matthew tapped Mona on the shoulder.

'I've got a surprise for you,' he said.

Mona and her grandparents followed him out of the Big Top and past the other tents to a trailer smelling of hay and animals.

'Keep very quiet,' said the lion-trainer.

Inside the trailer was a big cage, where a lioness lay with her four cubs. She lifted her head and snarled at the strangers. Mona shivered. She didn't need the lion-trainer to tell her they shouldn't go any closer.

The cubs were only as big as guinea pigs, with spotty golden-brown fur. Their eyes were shut tight; they were blind and helpless – and Mona wanted to hold one more than she'd ever wanted anything in her whole life. It was hard to believe they were going to grow up to be fierce, roaring lions like the ones she'd just seen in the Big Top.

But the lioness was glaring, her teeth and eyes bright in the darkness as she warned them all to keep away. All Mona could do was stand outside the cage and think how she would love them if she only had the chance.

CHAPTER 4

The next morning, the lion cages were loaded onto trucks. There was no time to waste: the circus was moving on to the next town and the next show.

In the cage, the mother lion was curled around her cubs. But the smallest cub was too weak to drink. The lioness stopped licking it. She had three healthy cubs and she needed to give them all her attention to make sure they survived.

Mona felt a little bit strange and a little bit special, being on holidays with her grandparents when all the other kids on the street still had another week

129

before school finished, so on the Saturday, Gran invited the girl next door over for lunch and a play.

Mona knew they could be friends from the way Sarah said hello to Heidi and the dogs.

'What I'd really love is a kitten,' said Sarah, 'but Mum and Dad always say no.'

'So do mine,' said Mona.

'Never mind,' said Gran, shooing the sausage dogs from under her feet as she carried a plate of sandwiches to the table. 'You never know what'll turn up around here!'

The phone rang. Grandpa answered it, and hung up looking puzzled. 'There's something at the airport for Mona. We've got to pick it up right away.'

'Cool!' said Sarah. 'I've never been to the airport.'

They sang 'We're Going to the Zoo' all the way in the car, because no one knew a song about going to the airport. Mona felt fizzy with wondering what the mystery parcel could be. She had no idea who it could be from.

Maybe Uncle Matthew's forgotten he gave me the circus tickets for Christmas, and has sent me stilts, she decided as Grandpa parked outside the freight terminal. Her uncle had given her juggling balls last year, soft red-and-yellow ones filled with seed, like the ones he used to practise. Stilts wouldn't fit into a letterbox. The parcel must be so long it was getting in people's way.

The more she thought about stilts, the more she wanted them. She could learn to dance on them the way Uncle Matthew did, and maybe she'd join the circus too when she grew up.

'I'll let you have a go, too,' she told Sarah.

'A go of what? How do you know what it is?' Sarah asked.

'You'll see. I've figured it out,' said Mona.

'Am I glad to see you!' said the man in the freight terminal. 'I didn't know what I was going to do if you didn't turn up.' He disappeared to the back of the building.

Mona felt confused. The terminal was huge. Stilts couldn't take up that much room! Her grandparents looked more and more worried.

The man came back carrying a cardboard box, and a cat carry-cage. In it, nestled in a blanket, was a tiny lion cub.

CHAPTER 5

he cub woke up and squawked. Mona knelt in front of its cage as it crawled out of its blankets, its milky eyes blinking.

'The poor baby!' Gran exclaimed.

'What was Matthew thinking?' said Grandpa.

Mona opened the door and picked up the cub. It nuzzled against her, sucking her fingers with its raspy tongue.

'We'll have to get it home and feed it before we can figure out what to do,' said Gran. She took the blanket out of the cage and helped Mona wrap up the cub. 'Now it'll feel safe, and keep you safe from scratches!'

'You'd never scratch me, would you?' Mona whispered to the bundle's furry head. She was sure she could hear a purr of an answer.

'Is it really a lion?' Sarah asked.

'It's really a lion,' said Grandpa. He didn't sound happy. 'We'd better check the box in case there's a tiger in there!'

But the cardboard box had three baby bottles, five tins of milk-formula powder, a bag of kitty litter – and a letter.

To my favourite niece!

I know how much you wanted to hold a lion cub, but I bet you never thought you'd be taking one home for Christmas!

The problem is that the lioness didn't have enough milk for all the cubs. This little girl was the smallest so she never got enough. The lion-trainer was afraid she was going to die because it will be very hard to go on hand-rearing her while we're travelling all over the country. I thought about Gran raising the little

goat last year, and I knew she'd want to
help you give this cub the same chance.

Love,

Uncle Matthew

Mona knew her grandparents were cross with
Uncle Matthew, because they always said that no
one should ever give someone else a pet without
asking first. But all she could think was, *I've got
my very own lion!*

'Wow,' Sarah said. 'I never knew anyone else
who got a lion for Christmas.'

'Neither did I!' said Grandpa, and began to
laugh. After a moment Gran started, and then
Sarah and Mona couldn't stop.

'What did you think it was going to be?' Sarah
asked, as they got into the car.

'Stilts,' said Mona, and that started everyone
laughing again.

'What are you going to call her?' Sarah asked.

'Kiki,' said Mona. She didn't have to think

about it – the name had been waiting there since she was two years old and had played at being a kitty called Kiki.

And if I name this lion, she thought, *she'll belong to me* – because she had never wanted anything as badly as she wanted to keep this tiny, helpless cub.

Her grandmother smiled and tickled the little lion under her chin. 'Hello, Kiki!'

Sweet as honey, relief rushed through Mona's body. It dissolved the tight worry-band around her chest until her whole body was as relaxed as the cub that was drifting off to sleep on her lap.

When they got home to Rainbow Street, Grandpa shut all the dogs outside so that nothing would disturb the cub's first feed in her new home.

Mona didn't want to let go of her for an instant. She carried her into the kitchen and sat cross-legged on the floor. Sarah slid down beside her, gently stroking Kiki's velvety head while Gran mixed up the milk formula.

She poured it into a baby bottle and showed the girls how to test the temperature by dripping a few drops onto the inside of their wrists. 'If it feels just a little bit warm, it'll be the right temperature for a baby animal,' she said.

Kiki was still sound asleep. Mona tickled her mouth with the bottle, and the tiny cub just wrinkled her nose and grunted. But when some of the warm milk dripped into her mouth, she finally began to suck.

When the bottle was empty Gran lifted Kiki off Mona's lap and rubbed her back till they heard a baby-lion burp.

'That feels better, doesn't it?' Gran murmured, carrying the cub over to the kitty-litter tray and helping her go to the toilet, which is what baby animals do after they've been fed.

Grandpa had already cut the cardboard box down to be a two-week-old lion-cub bed. Mona folded Kiki's blanket to fit in the bottom and lifted her in. In a minute the cub was asleep again.

She slept through Sarah's dad coming in to pick Sarah up and exclaiming three times, 'You've got to be kidding!' when he saw what was in the kitchen. She slept through the dogs being allowed in one by one to sniff the box, so they knew that the animal inside was a friend they mustn't chase.

She slept through Gran pulling Mona onto her lap and saying, 'We'll all do our best for Kiki. But her mother stopped feeding her because she didn't think she could keep her alive, and the lion-trainer let Matthew send her to us because he didn't think he could either. It's not going to be easy.'

'You kept Heidi alive when no one else could,' said Mona.

'And I'll do my best for Kiki,' Gran promised.

'But what's best for Kiki will change as she gets older,' Grandpa warned. 'And I don't know what your parents are going to say about a pet lion.'

Mona knew that he meant her parents would say no. But she was sure that once her parents met Kiki, they'd love her as much as she did.

CHAPTER 6

The first week that Kiki lived with the McNeils, she was sleepy and hungry. She needed a bottle every two hours, even at night, because she couldn't drink very much at one time. But soon she started to grow. She drank more and didn't need her bottle so often. She started crawling faster and further. Soon she could stand on wobbly legs, and started being able to see.

The baby bottle was nearly as big as the cub, but Kiki liked to lie back in Mona's arms and help hold it between her paws. Her eyes closed dreamily, her tummy getting rounder and rounder as the bottle got emptier.

'Greedy guts!' Mona teased, feeling as full of love as Kiki was full of milk.

Sometimes, if they were sitting on the back steps, Heidi would rest her head on Mona's knees, looking on as if she remembered being a tiny kid having her own bottle. When the cub was finished, and Mona put her down on the grass, the goat would nuzzle her gently.

Mona was glad that Kiki and Heidi were making friends. Having a lion cub for a pet was the best thing that had ever happened to her, but she knew a grown-up lion might eat a goat. 'You wouldn't do that, would you?' she whispered in Kiki's ear. 'You're my sweet baby lion. You'd never hurt your friends.'

Kiki's raspy tongue licked her face with a promise.

Frieda and Vicky, the sausage dogs, lived mostly inside the house. They sniffed Kiki hello every morning, and never snapped if she bumped into them, but when Mona was holding the cub they whined and poked their heads between her knees, their dark eyes shining jealously.

Gran didn't think the dogs would hurt the helpless cub, but she never left them alone together, just in case.

By the time Kiki was four weeks old she was nearly as big as the sausage dogs. She could walk on all four legs, wobbling proudly across the floor instead of creeping on her belly. She followed the family around the house, calling them with a scratchy noise that sounded like a frog meowing.

Mona took her outside to play on the grass and see the other dogs. They usually ignored her, because she wasn't old enough to play, but Heidi always stayed close by her side.

'Heidi thinks she's Kiki's babysitter,' Mona told Sarah.

It was true: the little nanny goat was determined to look after the lion cub.

Sarah came to see Kiki nearly every day. Sometimes she brought other friends, and then they brought their brothers and sisters and more friends. Finally Gran had to make a rule that only two children could come at a time.

'Kiki's still a baby,' she explained. 'She needs naps!'

Some visitors brought toys for Kiki: cat toys or special lion-cub toys they'd made themselves. That was useful, because as Kiki got older she wanted to play. The more she grew, the more she played, and the stronger she became, the rougher she played. None of her toys lasted for long.

When her teeth started growing, sharp and sore through her gums, she wanted to chew all the time. She couldn't understand why it was okay to chew a rubber bone but not Grandpa's best shoes.

'No, Kiki, no!' Mona said when she found her Barbie doll's arm chewed off at the elbow. The lion meowed, her round ears twitching as Mona put the doll on the top of the bookcase.

Mona's crossness melted. She knelt and rubbed noses with the cub. 'I love you way more than a Barbie doll.'

Gran had looked after lots of baby animals, but never a lion. She didn't know whether she should be feeding Kiki meat as well as milk, or what else they should be doing to look after her.

'Why don't we ask the zoo?' said Grandpa.

'NO!' shouted Mona. 'They might want to take her!'

'We have to find out what's best for Kiki,' said Gran. 'No matter what happens.'

So they went to see a veterinarian at the City Zoo. She gave them the milk formula that Kiki needed, and said that the cub wouldn't be ready to start eating meat till she was about ten weeks old. She said to call right away if Kiki ever got sick.

But she also said that lions couldn't live with people forever.

'Because they're not just big pussy-cats, they're wild animals,' Gran reminded Mona that night as the cub snuggled into the girl's lap with her bed-time bottle.

'Kiki's different!' Mona protested, burying her face in the lion's soft fur. 'She'd never be wild!'

Gran stroked Mona's dark hair and didn't answer.

CHAPTER 7

iki kept on growing. Her milky-blue eyes were turning golden brown. By the time she was six weeks old she was as big as a grown-up cat.

But she was still a baby. She slept all night in her box in the kitchen. When Mona picked her up in the morning, the cub was always sound asleep, warm and floppy.

'Hello, Sleepyhead,' Mona teased, rubbing her face against the lion's. She carried her out to the litter tray in the garden. The cub did what she was supposed to, then yawned and stumbled back so sleepily that Mona laughed, and picked her up again.

'Are you awake enough for breakfast?' Mona asked.

Kiki smelled the milk and squawked excitedly. Her voice still sounded more like a frog than a lion. She grabbed for the bottle with both paws, patting it happily as she sucked. It didn't take long to feed her now.

Buck the collie taught her to play chasey and wrestling games. Kiki liked that even more than ball games with Mona, because Buck let her climb all over him and somersault off his back.

Heidi played with them too, but sometimes she had to butt the dog and lion to remind them that she didn't like wrestling.

Uncle Matthew phoned when Kiki was nearly seven weeks old. 'How's the cub?' he asked.

'She's beautiful!' exclaimed Mona.

'Are you training her?' he asked.

'She always comes when she's called,' Mona said proudly.

'She'll be the best trained circus lioness ever!' said Uncle Matthew.

For a second, Mona wondered if she'd heard him right.

'Kiki is *never* going to be a circus lion!' she

cried. And Mona hung up on her favourite uncle. She remembered Kiki's father sitting on his stool, roaring at the lion-trainer. That roar was inside her now, a red rage bursting to get out.

She scooped the cub into her arms, holding her as tight as she could. But Kiki wasn't in a cuddling mood; she scrabbled to get down, and her back claws scratched Mona's left arm as she jumped.

It was a big scratch, and it bled a lot. Mona felt so muddled – so hurt, angry, sad and afraid – that she burst out howling.

Her grandmother came running. Her face turned white when she saw the blood on Mona's arm and T-shirt.

'She didn't mean to!' Mona cried, trying to wipe her tears away and smearing blood all over her face instead.

'I know. The problem is that she's a lion and doesn't know how strong she is.' Gran cleaned the scratch with antiseptic before covering it up with a bandage. 'What did Uncle Matthew have to say?'

'He wants Kiki to go back to the circus when she's big.'

'No way,' said Gran.

Mona stopped crying and breathed out, a long deep sigh of relief.

'But he's not completely wrong,' said Gran. 'You know you can't take her home with you. And Kiki's just shown us why she can't live with us forever.'

CHAPTER 8

Grandpa had made Kiki a scratching post when she was a few weeks old so she could sharpen her claws on that instead of the couch. He covered it with a scrap of carpet, because that's how cats like their scratching posts.

But Kiki was not a kitten, and her claws would grow bigger than any cat's. She chewed and clawed the post when she couldn't think of anything else to do, but she liked real wood better.

A few days after Uncle Matthew phoned, she chewed chunks out of one kitchen table leg. Gran thought it was funny. She was going to tell people that the table had been carved by a lion.

But that's not what she told Kiki: 'Naughty

lion!' said Gran. 'Go outside till you can be good!'

Kiki stalked out to the garden and started scratching the bark of a big magnolia tree. Bark under her claws was even better than a polished table leg.

Suddenly she saw a possum in the branches above her. Kiki was much too young to hunt, even if she'd had a mother lion to teach her, but she knew she wanted to chase the possum.

She pulled herself up onto a low branch.

The possum was sound asleep.

The lion cub scratched and climbed higher. The possum woke up and stared. Kiki climbed to a higher branch.

The possum disappeared into the top of the tree. Kiki couldn't see him but she pulled herself up onto the next branch anyway.

Gran had told Mona to wait before she followed Kiki out to the garden, because she wanted the cub to remember that she'd been naughty. It felt like a long three minutes before Mona could grab a ball and go out to play with her.

'Kiki!' she called, waiting for the cub to come

rushing, rubbing her head against Mona's knees with happy lion grunts.

Frieda and Vicky looked up from their afternoon nap in the sunny living room. Freckles and Buck came running from different snoozing spots in the garden, in case Mona was going to feed Kiki something delicious. Only Goldie, too deaf to hear, went on sleeping.

But Kiki was nowhere to be seen.

'KIKI!' Mona shouted.

A growly meow came from the magnolia tree. Mona had never heard Kiki make exactly that sound before, but she knew it was a frightened noise. She looked up and saw Kiki lying on a high branch, with her legs dangling over either side.

Mona raced to the bottom of the tree. 'How did you get up there?'

'Meow!' said Kiki.

Mona was pretty sure it was a *Don't ask how I got up here – just get me down!* meow.

Mona started to climb. The magnolia tree was her favourite climbing tree, but she'd never gone as high as the branch where Kiki was now. It didn't look strong enough to hold her.

149

She scrambled up to the branch below and caught her breath. Holding the trunk with one arm, she reached towards the cub. She could almost touch her – nearly, but not quite. 'Come on, Kiki,' Mona coaxed. 'Just wiggle backwards. I'll help you.'

'Mona!' Gran called. 'Can't you find Kiki?'

'Up here!' Mona shouted. 'I can't quite reach—'

The lion cub wriggled away from her, further along the branch.

'Kiki, stop!' Mona shouted, because now the thin end of the branch was sagging under the cub's weight. Kiki couldn't stop; she was slipping and sliding…and before Mona could say anything more, the cub was springing right off the thin whippy end of the branch. Straight into the neighbour's backyard.

Mona slipped backwards down the trunk as fast as she could, tearing her bandage and skinning her hands and knees.

'Are you all right?' her grandmother called.

'Kiki's in the Hoovers' yard!' Mona panted, sucking the blood off her hand.

Gran sprinted to the back fence. The fence

was tall, and Gran wasn't, but she pulled herself up and over like an acrobat in Uncle Matthew's circus. By the time Mona scrambled over behind her, her grandmother had already run through the garden and out the driveway.

The Hoovers were good neighbours. They probably wouldn't mind a lion cub in their yard just this once. The problem was that they didn't have a fence across the front of their garden. Kiki could run straight out of their yard and down the street. And frightened animals could run a long way.

Mona's heart pounded as she raced after her grandmother. She was too breathless even to shout the name pounding in her head: *Kiki! Kiki!*

But a frightened lion cub knows that it's safer to hide than run, and Kiki had hidden in the first place she saw. Out of the corner of her eye, Mona spotted tawny fur under the big blue flowers of a hydrangea bush.

Kiki was so afraid she didn't recognise Mona at first. For those few moments, she was a wild animal, with her eyes wide and her ears flattened back.

Mona knew that the terrified cub could scratch without knowing what she was doing. She lay quietly on the ground in front of the bush, murmuring things Kiki liked to hear.

Finally the cub's breathing settled, her eyes calmed, and she let Mona pat her. Then she crawled out to be rescued, and became a pet again.

When Grandpa came home from work, he cut off every branch in the yard that dangled over a neighbour's fence.

CHAPTER 9

Kiki was growing every day: bigger, stronger and braver. She loved jumping on the vacuum cleaner when Gran was cleaning the house. She loved chasing balls with anyone who'd throw or kick one for her. And she absolutely loved chewing huge bones.

Her favourite game was standing on her hind legs to grab old Goldie's tail with her front paws, and walking around behind him. When the golden retriever was bored with the game, he just sat down on her – and when he got up again, Kiki left him alone for a while.

Her second-favourite game was jumping out at Mona and her grandparents from behind the couch. Once she leapt on Mona's back so hard that she knocked her down. No one else saw and Mona didn't tell.

But then she knocked over Sarah's little brother, face-down onto the back step. His chin gushed so much blood that, he had to have two stitches. After that, Sarah wasn't allowed to come over to play anymore. Mona had to talk to her over the fence and hold Kiki up for Sarah to pat. And Kiki was getting too heavy for Mona to lift.

But when the cub lay on her back to have her tummy rubbed, looking up at Mona through dreamy half-closed eyes, a wriggly worm of happiness twisted inside Mona. She thought she would never love anything as much as she loved this little lion.

Uncle Matthew phoned again.

'Kiki's not going to be in the circus!' Mona said.

'None of the cubs are,' said her uncle. 'The lion-trainer's going to retire when these lions are too old to perform. Kiki's sisters are going to a zoo.'

154

'A zoo!' Mona exclaimed.

'The lion enclosure is fantastic. They'll love it!'

'Maybe,' said Mona.

'You should send Kiki there too,' said Uncle Matthew. 'It sounds like you've done a great job of raising her, Mona, but she'd be better off living with other lions instead of people and dogs – and the goat.'

'Kiki loves us!' Mona shouted. 'She's not going to the zoo!'

Now Mona couldn't pretend any longer that her mother and father would let her take a lion home. It was like wishing she could grow wings and fly. It was impossible.

'Can Kiki stay with you when I go home?' she asked her grandmother.

'I wish she could,' Gran said, hugging Mona close. 'I wish she could stay little, and cute and happy. I wish you could stay here forever too! But life doesn't work like that. Kiki's going to get bigger – and you're going to go back to your parents.'

'But I'll come back to visit! She'd still remember me!'

'It's not just about whether we can go on living with Kiki. Matthew's right to say that staying with us isn't fair to her – she's a lion, not a dog or goat. We all need to find out what we should do in our lives: Kiki's job is to find out how to be a lion.'

Mona buried her head under her pillow. She didn't want to hear any more.

That night Mona dreamed of golden hills rolling down to a wide blue lake. Zebras and antelope grazed, giraffes nibbled tall branches, hippos splashed in the water, and elephants trumpeted.

And there were lions. Magnificent, king-of-the-beast lions dozed under trees, sleek lionesses stalked through long grass, and playful cubs wrestled over logs. Mona was in the middle of them, rolling, growling and chasing with the tumble of young lions.

She looked down at her paws and realised she was a lion too. She was Kiki, wild and free in a place where she belonged.

Mona woke up in the morning feeling happy, even though nothing had changed since she'd cried under her pillow in the dark. But when she went out to the kitchen and greeted her sleeping cub, she remembered her dream.

'You were in Africa, Kiki!' she whispered. The cub's ears twitched as Mona told her, 'There were hills, and animals, and a blue waterhole.'

'We should find out how she can get there,' said Gran.

'It was just a dream!' said Mona.

'Sometimes we have to follow our dreams,' said Gran.

CHAPTER 10

ona's new dream was to send Kiki back to Africa, because that's where lions come from. Gran and Grandpa helped her phone or write letters to whoever might know how to help.

Everyone told them the same thing: they couldn't send Kiki straight to Africa, because she wouldn't have her own family. Instead, they could take her to a safari park, where she could be safe and almost free.

The best safari park was nearly halfway between her grandparents' house in Rainbow Street and the city where Mona lived with her parents.

So Mona wrote a letter.

Dear Park People,

I have a lion cub named Kiki. She is very
smart and loving. She's very well behaved,
but she needs to live with other lions. I
would like her to go to Africa so she could
be free, but if she can't do that I hope she
can go to live in your park. I know that
everyone in your park would love her.

Yours truly, Mona McNeil

Four days later she got a big envelope in the mail.
Inside was a letter and a brochure showing wide
hills and trees, with lions dozing and giraffes
grazing.

Dear Mona,

The only way that Kiki could go to
Africa is if we had several other female
cubs her age so that they could form
their own pride, to learn how to hunt and
live in the wild together.

```
    Unfortunately, we don't have any
female cubs roughly the same age as Kiki.
    However, we'd be delighted to have her
come and live with us. We believe she will
be safe and happy, and we know we
will love her.

    Yours sincerely,

    Karhy Harris,
    Safari Park Manager
```

'It looks like a beautiful place,' Gran said, studying the brochure.

'She'll be well looked after,' said Grandpa.

The lump in Mona's throat was too big for her to answer. She knew this was the best place for Kiki to go. She just wished she'd never dreamed of something even better.

A week later, they started out on the long journey to take Kiki to her new home and Mona back to her old one.

Kiki was twelve weeks old. She was as big as a

medium-sized dog, and she loved riding in the car. Mona laughed out loud at the surprised *Ohs!* on people's faces as they drove past and saw a lion staring out the window.

Late that afternoon, they pitched their tent in a 'Dogs Allowed' campground. The sign didn't say anything about lions.

Mona clipped a leash onto Kiki's collar. She wanted the cub to run with her, but the more she tugged, the harder Kiki tugged back and growled, her ears flattened to her head.

'Sorry, Kiki!' Mona said sadly.

She got a ball out of the car. Kiki's ears twitched forward again – it was her favourite blue ball. Grandpa changed the leash for a long rope that Kiki couldn't feel pulling on her collar, and Mona and her lion played a crazy ball game in a circle around him.

That night Mona lay awake as long as she could. She wanted to burn every minute with Kiki into her memory so that it would be there forever. She snuggled her sleeping-bag around the lion cub's bed. Kiki grunted lovingly and fell asleep sucking Mona's thumb.

They left early in the morning before the sun was up and the other campers were awake. Mona and Kiki curled up in the back seat and let the car rock them back to sleep.

When Mona woke up they were parked in front of a set of tall gates, with a sign: WILDLIFE SAFARI PARK. Grandpa was talking to a man at the gate, and a smiling woman in a khaki uniform was coming towards them.

'Welcome, Kiki!' she said. 'I'm Kathy.'

Mona's hands were shaking, and her insides felt as if they were being ripped in two. *I've changed my mind!* she wanted to shout. *I can't leave her here all alone!*

But she didn't say it. Even if she could talk her parents into moving next door to the safari park, it wouldn't be fair to Kiki. The cub wouldn't know if she was a wild animal or a pet.

She wiped away her hot tears and got out of the car with her lion.

'I've got good news for you,' Kathy said, rubbing behind the cub's ears the way Kiki especially loved. 'I talked to the City Zoo yesterday. They'd just been offered three lioness cubs from a circus – but they've agreed to send them here instead, to see if they can form a pride with Kiki.'

'They're her sisters!' Mona exclaimed. 'Kiki, you're going to see your sisters again!'

'Perfect!' said Kathy. 'Because if they're together, they've all got a chance to be set free.'

'In Africa?' Mona asked.

'Yes – a wonderful sanctuary in Zambia. It has a program of teaching cubs born in zoos how to be wild again. Kiki's a lucky little lioness: she'll be safe, but completely free, where she belongs.'

Mona nodded. Tears were leaking out faster than she could stop them. She couldn't speak; she hadn't known that anything could hurt this much.

'Meow?' Kiki squawked, and stood up on her hind legs to wrap her front paws tightly around Mona. Mona hugged her back, with her face against the cub's neck and the tears soaking into the golden fur.

'Goodbye,' Mona whispered.

CHAPTER 11

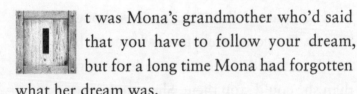

It was Mona's grandmother who'd said that you have to follow your dream, but for a long time Mona had forgotten what her dream was.

Now, as she sat on the worn front step of the old house in Rainbow Street, feeding handfuls of grass to the three-legged goat, she turned back into an eight-year-old girl and could almost smell spilled milk and love again. Of course she knew that this goat wasn't Heidi, because Heidi had gone with her grandparents when they moved across the country to live closer to Mona and her mum and dad, and had lived to be a very old goat. Just like she knew that she wasn't a little girl anymore, but a grown-up woman who had to decide what to do with her life.

And suddenly, she knew exactly what that was. She wanted to make the house into a home for animals, the way it had been when her grandparents lived there. Though not exactly like that, because Mona wanted to help lots of animals, more animals than she could have as pets, even in this house with a big garden. She wanted to help all the animals that needed help.

The goat nibbled hopefully at her sandals till she rubbed under his chin, down to his armpits. He nodded happily, just like Heidi used to.

'Would you be scared of a baby lion?' Mona asked him.

The goat burped.

'I didn't think so,' said Mona. 'Neither was Heidi.'

An old man carrying a bag of cabbage and lettuce leaves came up the path. The goat turned away from Mona and trotted eagerly towards him.

'I see you've met Fred,' said the old man. 'And I'm Bert. Fred and I are mates from way back.'

The goat butted the bag till Bert fed him a cabbage leaf. 'I've been coming over to see him since the people living here left,' he explained. 'If I had a house and garden I'd take him home with me. But I don't think he'd like living in a flat!'

'Poor Fred,' said Mona, though the goat looked very happy with cabbage leaf sticking out of both sides of his mouth. 'What happened to his leg?'

'He got out when he was a kid, and was hit by a car. It doesn't seem to bother him.'

Fred butted the bag again and started munching on a lettuce leaf.

'My grandparents loved goats,' said Mona. 'They moved away a long time ago, but this house had too many happy memories to sell it.'

'And the happy memories were yours too?' asked Bert.

Mona nodded. 'That's why they decided that when the last people moved out, the house would belong to me.'

'Would it be okay if I still come to look after Fred?' asked Bert.

'I think Fred would like that,' said Mona.

'And so would I. Gran said they were giving me the house so I could follow my dream. I've just figured out what that is.'

So the next day, Mona went back to the city where she'd lived for so long. She quit her job and packed up her flat. And then she flew back across the country to start making her new life.

She found a new place to live, not far from Rainbow Street. Then she went to the City Animal Shelter in the middle of town.

Mona took a deep breath and opened the front door. She walked past the kennels and cages. There were big dogs, small dogs, curly haired dogs, smooth spotty dogs; white, gold, brown and black dogs. There were delicate kitties and fluffy cats. There were lop-eared bunnies and floppy-haired guinea pigs.

Mona tried not to look. Now that she knew exactly what her dream was, she didn't know what she was going to do if she couldn't make it come true.

She took the lift up to the offices on the top floor. Her hands were shaking as she knocked.

She'd been to business meetings before. She'd just never been to one that could change her whole life.

A receptionist with polished fingernails showed her in to an office where a man and two women in suits were sitting on the other side of a long table. Mona sat down across from them.

'I want to turn my grandparents' house into an animal shelter,' she explained. 'And I want the job of running it.'

'You need more than one person to run an animal shelter,' said one of the women.

'I've already got one volunteer,' said Mona. 'As well as a resident goat.'

The people in suits looked at each other. 'We do need another shelter,' the other woman said at last. 'There isn't enough room here for all the animals that need help.'

'There'll be a lot of things to work out,' the man warned.

'It's not like having your own pets at home,' the first woman explained. 'You'll start to love some of the animals – but you have to give them up when they find the right home.'

'I learned how to do that a long time ago,' said Mona.

The City Animal Shelter sent painters and carpenters to help Mona turn the Rainbow Street house into a proper animal shelter.

The reception area, where Mona would meet the animals that came in, had chairs and a big desk. On the wall was a photograph of Kiki and her cubs in the wildlife sanctuary in Zambia. Kiki had learned all the things her mother would have taught her if she'd been born in the wild, and now she was living free.

Across the hall was the examination room, for the visiting veterinarian to check the animals, and the surgery to treat the sick ones. There were rooms with cages for small animals like pet rats and guinea pigs.

The house was pale blue, just as it had been when Mona was a girl, but the door was a cheery, cherry red. Over the door, Mona painted a bright, seven-coloured rainbow.

The grand opening of the Rainbow Street Shelter should have been a bright and beautiful day, with sunshine, blue skies and singing birds. Instead, rain tumbled down, thunder thundered, and lightning flashed in the black sky.

'Maybe it'll stop by the time they all get here,' Bert said hopefully.

Everyone was coming at ten o'clock: the mayor, the people from the City Animal Shelter, photographers, reporters – and best of all, lots of people who cared about animals.

The rain didn't stop.

Bert tied a ribbon across the front gate.

A newspaper photographer drove up. He got out of his car and stepped into a puddle. There were no crowds of people, just a young woman, an old man and a three-legged goat huddled under an umbrella. The photographer got back into his car and drove away.

The mayor, his assistant and the people from the City Animal Shelter arrived a minute later. The mayor waited for a journalist to get out of her car, then smiled and snipped the soggy ribbon. They all raced down the path to the front door.

'Congratulations,' said the mayor, shaking Mona and Bert's hands.

Mona showed them around the building. They looked through the windows at the outside enclosures and said what a good job she'd done. They thanked Mona for donating the building and said they looked forward to working with her.

Then they scurried back through the raindrops to their cars. Mona and Bert stood at the gate to watch them drive away.

It wasn't how Mona had imagined the first day of her dream.

'Look!' said Bert.

A bedraggled white cockatoo was flapping wearily towards them. Flying low over their heads, with its left wing drooping, it landed in the tree near the red front door. It looked wet, miserable and lost.

'G'day, mate,' Bert called softly.

The bird cocked its head warily.

'He's scared,' said Mona. 'He doesn't look like he's used to flying.'

He's hungry,' said Bert. 'Hold on, mate, you've come to the right place for a treat!'

Mona waited at the gate as Bert walked slowly around the garden to the back of the house. Whether the bird had escaped from a cage or was a wild bird who'd been injured, he needed help now.

'You look like you've travelled a long way,' she told him. 'We should call you Gulliver – at least till you find your own home.'

Then the rain stopped. The sun came out, and for a moment Mona stood blinking in the brightness.

When she could see again, Bert was standing in front of the blue house with the wet cockatoo eating birdseed from his hand.

Above them was a rainbow.

Buster the Hero Cat

CHAPTER 1

Buster and his brother and sisters were born in a box at the back of a garage. The other four kittens were fluffy and pretty: his sisters were grey and his brother was black. But Buster had a square head with a crooked white snip on his nose. His fur was as orange as marmalade on warm toast.

Their mother licked them clean, fed them, and looked after them so well that their cardboard box was as good a home as the comfiest cat basket a kitten could have. All the time the kittens were growing – opening their eyes to look around, and learning to wash their faces and paws clean with their small pink tongues – the mother cat kept them secret and safe.

One day, when the kittens were just old enough to walk and tumble and play, the mother cat led them out of the box to explore the world beyond the garage. But as each tiny kitten came blinking out into its first bright sunlight, a hand grabbed them and dumped them into a big bag. The mother cat yowled and the kittens mewed, but the bag was dropped into a car and the mother cat was left behind.

The car drove down a long road while the frightened kittens squirmed in the dark, squeezy bag. Then they felt a *whoosh!* as the bag was tossed from the car, and a *thump!* as they landed on the grass beside the road.

No one saw it happen, and so no one ever knew who had done such a cruel and terrible thing.

But Buster knew, and for the rest of his life he hated going in cars or being anywhere squeezy where he couldn't get out, and he hated people wearing orange caps.

Luckily, the next person who drove down the road that day was Eliza Jones, and she was a very different sort of person. Even more luckily, she saw the squirming bag. She didn't know what was inside, but she knew if it was squirming it must be alive, and if it was alive it didn't belong in a bag on the side of the road. Even though the bag squirmed so much that she was afraid it might be a snake, she stopped her car and walked slowly towards it.

As she got closer, she heard a chorus of mewing.

Eliza sprinted to the bag and ripped it open. She was so angry at whoever had dumped the kittens, so sad for how scared they were, and so happy that she'd found them, that she wanted to take them all home and give them enough love and kindness they'd forget just how frightened they'd been.

But she knew that one kitten was enough for her tiny apartment, so in the end she drove straight to the Rainbow Street Shelter.

CHAPTER 2

liza Jones ran through the cherry-red door, under the seven-coloured rainbow of the animal shelter.

'Can I help you?' called Gulliver, the cockatoo, just as Mona opened the door to ask the same thing.

Eliza Jones told Mona the story of finding the kittens. She was still angry and sad as she told it. So was Mona when she heard it.

'Of course we'll look after the kittens!' she said, and went out to the car with Eliza.

'This is the one I'm keeping,' said Eliza, picking up Buster's handsome black brother.

Mona gathered up the other kittens. Three pretty fluffy grey kittens mewed and snuggled

177

into her arms. The orange kitten with a square head scratched and leapt out of the car.

Mona put the other kittens down again and raced after Buster. 'Here, kitty, kitty!' she called.

Eliza Jones raced after her. 'Here, puss, puss!'

Buster didn't listen. He raced down Rainbow Street and across someone's front lawn. A big dog roared at him from behind a fence, and Buster raced up the nearest tree. It was a huge old oak tree, the tallest tree on the block.

Mona and Eliza looked up, and up. 'Meow,' they heard, from high in the tree.

Mona began to climb. She'd been rescuing animals since she was eight years old, and sometimes climbing trees was the only way to do it. She scrambled up to Buster's branch, and coaxed and cooed till he wiggled close enough for her to grab him and take him safely down.

The man in the house behind the oak tree took a picture of Mona rescuing the kitten, and sent it to the newspaper.

People who wanted a cat came to the Rainbow Street Shelter to see the feisty orange kitten they'd read about in the newspaper, but when they got there they saw Buster's pretty, fluffy sisters. 'What adorable kittens!' they always said – and one after the other, Buster's three sisters went home with new families.

Buster was still not pretty or fluffy. He got taller and more orange, and he waited to know people before he decided if he liked them. Mona and Bert were the only people he trusted. Gradually he began to let them pat him. Every day, they were allowed to stroke him for a little bit longer, until one morning Bert picked him up and cuddled him. A strange rumble came from the little cat's chest.

'Did you hear that?' Bert asked Mona. 'He's purring!'

They felt like having a party. Knowing that the kitten was happy again was the best 'thank you' they could ever have for working in the shelter.

But Buster had added big barking dogs to the list of things he didn't like, and nothing was going to change his mind about that.

When Buster grew into a yowly, prowly, tall and rangy teenage orange kitten, a family took

179

him home. Buster wouldn't sit on their laps, and he wouldn't stop chasing their dog, so after three days they took him back to Rainbow Street.

'Sorry, Buster,' said Mona. 'Maybe you'd better stay here and live with us, like Gulliver.'

But deep down, Mona kept hoping that Buster would find his very own home. 'The right people must be somewhere!' she said to Bert.

Finally, the right person came.

Mr Larsen was very old, and he didn't want a brand-new, fluffy kitten.

'I don't care what colour it is or what it looks like,' he said. 'But I'll know when I meet the cat that's right for me.'

Then he saw Buster, lying in the sun on the roof of his cat-kennel. Buster looked back at Mr Larsen for a long minute. Then he jumped down, arched his back and stretched, and stalked over to meet the old man.

'A marmalade cat!' said Mr Larsen. 'I've always wanted a marmalade cat!'

'Buster hasn't had an easy life,' said Mona. 'He's got a bit of an attitude.'

'Then he's the cat for me!' said Mr Larsen.

CHAPTER 3

ust as Mr Larsen knew that Buster was exactly the right cat for him, Josh knew that Rex was exactly the right rabbit for him.

Rex was a big rabbit with velvety orange fur. When he was younger he had liked playing with a little red ball and exploring new parts of the garden: once he'd even chased a stray cat out of the Lee's yard. Now Rex was old but sometimes he still felt so good that he did crazy hopping bunny dances, jumping and twisting around the floor with Josh and Mai copying him. And when he was tired, he liked lying on his back and having his tummy stroked till he went to sleep.

If Josh was sad he always started to feel better again when Rex sat on his lap and let Josh stroke him, from behind the twitchy ears right down to the tail. Sometimes Josh thought there was something magic in Rex's soft fur, which made bad things seem not so terrible.

Rex wasn't just Josh's rabbit; Mrs Lee had him before she even met Mr Lee. Then they got married, and then Mai was born, and then Josh, and now Rex was everyone's pet.

He had his own hutch to sleep in. For warm sunny days he had a cage in the backyard that Josh and Mai moved around so he always had a fresh patch of grass to nibble. On cold rainy days he stayed inside and lollopped around the family room and kitchen. When he was inside he had a litter-tray in the laundry, and he never had an accident... Except for the time he ate the cable to the computer modem, and the time he ate the mobile phone charger cord, but those were a different kind of accident. 'Bunnies make mistakes like everyone else,' said Josh's mum.

Rex never made those sorts of mistakes any more. In the last few months, Rex had changed.

He still sometimes liked his tummy being stroked and tickled, but he lolloped so slowly it was barely a bounce, and he never danced now. He didn't do anything much except sleep and nibble.

But he was part of the Lees' family, and Josh loved him.

Buster was still young. He was two years old, and he'd lived with Mr Larsen for more than half his life. He still hated orange caps, cars, squeezy places and big dogs, but he'd found lots more things that he liked.

He liked going for walks, even though Mr Larsen made him wear a harness and a leash. He liked lying in the sun, and sitting on the verandah beside Mr Larsen. He liked tossing and chasing the long curls of carrot peel Mr Larsen dropped for him when he was making dinner. Most of all, he loved Mr Larsen.

And Mr Larsen thought Buster was the most perfect cat in the whole world.

The first time Josh saw Buster, the big marmalade cat and a very tall, very old man were walking home from the beach.

This was not a cute and fluffy kitty cat. It was the biggest cat Josh had ever seen, and people who didn't like cats might have even said he was ugly. He had a square head, with a crooked white snip on his nose, and one bent over ear that looked as if someone had taken a nibble out of the tip.

But he was exactly the same orange colour as Rex, and Josh thought that was the most perfect colour an animal-friend could be. He was also the only cat Josh had ever seen walking on a leash.

'I'd never catch him if I let him loose,' said the old man. 'He chases every dog he sees, right down the beach and back again. Dogs don't know what to do when they see Buster coming!'

Josh didn't see the cat again for a long time, but he liked to think about him. There was something wild and crazy about a giant cat that chased dogs, as if he was so brave that didn't even know that he was a cat.

Josh sometimes felt wild and crazy, but he didn't know if he was brave. He knew for sure that he wasn't big. Josh's dad was tall and strong. His big sister Mai looked like their dad. But Josh's mum was short and skinny, and Josh looked like their mum.

This year Mai was going to secondary school, and Josh had started walking to school by himself.

The Lees' house was on Spray Street. If you walked straight down their street for two blocks, then turned right for one block, you ended up at the Ocean Street corner where the schoolyard started. That was the way Mai always went.

Josh liked to turn right at the first corner to get to Ocean Street, and walk that way to the school. It was exactly the same distance and took him exactly the same time.

And it took him past the house where the very old man and the very large cat lived. Every morning as he walked to school he saw them sitting outside on the verandah in the sun.

The old man looked even older. Josh never saw him walking to the beach anymore, but he always waved as Josh walked by, and Josh waved back. The big cat sat beside him, watching everything and everyone, as if he was deciding whether or not they needed to be chased away.

Josh liked the way Buster sat there on guard beside his man. He thought he'd like having a pet who looked out for him like that, but then he felt mean, as if Rex might know what he was thinking, so the next day he walked the other way to school.

The day after that everything changed.

CHAPTER 4

Rex had had a very long life for a rabbit. He'd had a very happy life too. But Rex had lived as long as a bunny could possibly live, and he was so very, very old that when he went to sleep that night, snuggled up safe in his hutch, he never woke up again.

In the morning Josh found him curled up in the hay bed. He lay so completely still that Josh knew something wasn't right. Not even his nose was twitching. 'Wake up, Rex!' he shouted, but when he patted the soft orange fur, the rabbit's body was cold.

From that moment Josh felt as if part of his life had been ripped away. And it didn't matter how much everyone said what a happy life Rex had had, or that it was his time to go – the whole family was sad and nothing seemed right.

'It's hard to believe now,' said Mr Lee, 'but one day we'll be ready to get another pet.'

'Maybe a dog that we could take for walks on the beach,' said Mai.

'Or another baby bunny,' said Mrs Lee. 'You kids can't imagine how sweet Rex was when he was tiny.'

'I don't ever want another pet!' Josh shouted. 'I just want Rex!'

'We all do,' said his mum.

'There'll never be another Rex,' said his dad. 'But when we're ready to have another pet, we'll learn to love it too.'

Josh knew he'd never be ready. He didn't want to get used to another pet – and he never wanted to feel this sad again. It wasn't worth loving anything if it made you feel this bad when it died.

Now Josh didn't want to meet anyone with a pet. He walked the other way to school so he didn't have to see Mr Larsen and Buster. And he definitely didn't want to go to the next 'First Monday of the Month' assembly. That was when Hannah stood up in front of the whole school to do a presentation about a lost pet. Josh didn't know how she could do it; he didn't even like standing up in front of everyone in his class!

Josh had known Hannah since Year Two. She'd been talking about dogs for as long as he'd known her. On the first day of school this year Hannah told the class about the dog she'd found, and how her parents had made her take it to the Rainbow Street Shelter. And then the new boy had jumped out of his chair so fast he'd knocked his desk over. 'His name is Bear!' he'd shouted. 'He's my dog!'

Even though Hannah had her own puppy now, she still went to Rainbow Street every week to help feed the lost animals. She cleaned out their cages and played with them so they remembered how to trust people again. And every month, from that first assembly on the First Monday of the Month, she told the school about a pet who needed a home.

Josh knew for sure that hearing stories about homeless animals wasn't going to make him feel any better at all.

Maybe I'll catch a cold and be too sick to go to school on Monday, he thought. He started practising coughing.

CHAPTER 5

It was the scariest night of Buster's life. It was scarier than being dumped out of a car, being chased by big dogs or being stuck at the top of a tall tree.

It started just like every other night. Mr Larsen and Buster sat out on the verandah after dinner till it was dark, then went inside and watched TV till bedtime.

Watching TV was the only time Buster sat on Mr Larsen's lap. His purr started off as a whispery hum, but as the old man's hands stroked the thick fur from the top of his head down his back to the start of his tail, Buster's purr rumbled louder and louder. After a few minutes his whole body thrummed like a fishing boat heading out to sea.

At bedtime Mr Larsen made himself a mug of tea. He poured a bit of milk into Buster's saucer, and Buster twined lovingly around his legs. A splash of tea slopped onto the floor.

'That was a close one, Buster!' Mr Larsen said.

'Meow,' agreed Buster.

The old man turned to put the saucer down. He slipped in the spilled tea and crashed to the floor. Buster mewed and prowled around him, but Mr Larsen didn't move.

Buster didn't care about the spilled milk or the smashed saucer; he just wanted his man to wake up. He licked Mr Larsen's face, nudged his hands and yowled in his ear, over and over, until finally the old man opened his eyes.

Mr Larsen tried to sit up, and fell back down – but Buster kept on licking his face with his raspy tongue until Mr Larsen was ready to try again.

Slowly, slowly, with Buster nudging and yowling every time he went back to sleep, Mr Larsen woke up enough to get his mobile phone out of his pocket and dial 000.

When the ambulance came with its sirens and lights, Buster sat by his owner's head glaring at the people rushing into his house.

'It's okay, Buster,' Mr Larsen whispered.

Buster meowed with his ears flat and worried. He didn't think it looked okay at all.

'He saved my life,' Mr Larsen told the paramedics as they lifted him onto a stretcher.

'Good puss,' they said, and before they wheeled Mr Larsen out of the house, the paramedics shut Buster into the lounge room to keep him safe.

Buster paced around the empty room, yowling as if his heart would break.

The next day there was a story in the local newspaper:

Cat Saves Owner's Life!

A year-and-a-half ago, Mr Edward Larsen rescued a cat from the Rainbow Street Shelter.

Last night, the cat returned the favour by rescuing his elderly owner. Mr Larsen, aged 89, fell in his kitchen, breaking his hip and losing consciousness.

Our reporters interviewed Mr Larsen from his hospital bed. 'Buster wasn't going to let me die', Mr Larsen said. 'He licked my nose and yowled in my ears till I woke up enough to call 000. That cat is a hero!'

However, in a sad twist to the tale, when Mr Larsen's son arrived from Sydney, the cat was missing. He is described as a large orange tabby cat. Anyone seeing him is asked to phone the Rainbow Street Shelter.

As Buster prowled the lounge room that terrible night of flashing lights and screaming sirens, he noticed that one window was open a crack.

Buster was very good at figuring out whether he could fit through a space. He knew exactly how big his head and body were compared to any sort of hole or open window. And he knew that Mr Larsen never left a window open wide enough for him to jump out.

But Buster wasn't thinking – he was scared and desperate, and he wanted Mr Larsen.

Most cats that were scared and desperate would have hidden behind the couch or under a chair, but Buster wasn't most cats.

Buster leapt at the window. He didn't fit through the opening. Instead, he crashed right through the glass and landed on the lawn outside. He had one cut paw and a deep scratch across his head, but Buster didn't notice. He started to run.

He didn't know where he was going. He didn't know where Mr Larsen had gone, and he wasn't even trying to follow the ambulance: he was just running.

It was a long time before he stopped. When he did, he didn't know where he was.

CHAPTER 6

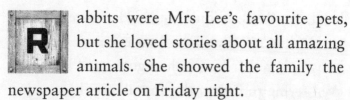abbits were Mrs Lee's favourite pets, but she loved stories about all amazing animals. She showed the family the newspaper article on Friday night.

'Buster!' said Josh. 'That's the big cat who's exactly the same colour Rex was!'

'Poor Mr Larsen,' said Mrs Lee. 'And poor Buster.'

'We've got to find him!' said Josh.

So the next morning, when Josh and his family walked to the beach, they went past Mr Larsen's house on the way.

Josh searched under bushes and into shadowy, cat-hidey corners. He peered through the high wire fence of the house that was being rebuilt next door.

'When did Mr Larsen go to hospital?' he asked his mum.

'Wednesday night,' she said. 'Wednesday till Saturday is a long time for a cat to go hungry.'

Josh thought about how he used to hold a carrot for Rex to nibble as a special treat. He thought about how they had always made sure Rex had clean water and pellets so he was never thirsty or hungry.

He knew that Mr Larsen would have looked after Buster the same way. But Mr Larsen couldn't look after Buster now because he was in hospital, and Josh's family didn't have Rex to look after. *It's just not fair!* thought Josh.

'Let's look for Buster instead of going to the beach,' he said.

'That's what I was going to say!' everyone else said together.

They looked up into trees and walked up and down the streets, around the block and the next block after that, but there was no sign of a giant marmalade cat.

Mrs Lee made Josh's favourite noodles for dinner that night, but Josh could hardly swallow them. He kept wondering if Buster had found anything to eat. He hated thinking about that brave, crazy cat being afraid, lost and starving.

But Buster was a smart cat. When he'd stopped running on that terrifying Wednesday night and realised he didn't know where he was, Buster found a quiet garden with fat bushes sprawling against the garage wall. He crawled in under the middle bush, scratched out a bed in the dirt, then curled up and slept for the rest of the night.

In the morning he sat up and groomed himself, combing the bits of broken glass off his head with his claws, and licking the dried blood off his paws. His rough sandpaper tongue smoothed out the fur along his back and his tail, and then he sat on his bottom, stretching his legs and curling between them to lick his belly and everywhere else.

Buster felt calmer when he was clean. He swaggered out of his camping place as if it had always belonged to him.

The first thing he saw was a small spotty dog

in the garden next door. The second thing was a woman putting a bowl down on the back step, and going back inside.

Buster was ready for breakfast. He jumped to the top of the fence and over to the step before the dog had time to see him. With a hiss and spit, Buster chased the little dog away from his bowl: dog food wasn't as tasty as cat food, but it was better than no breakfast at all.

The dog was so shocked at being chased by a cat that it quivered against the back fence for a minute before it started to bark.

'What's the matter, Patchie?' the woman called from inside the house.

Buster munched faster.

The woman opened the door.

'Get out of here!' she shouted, as Buster raced across the yard like an orange streak of lightning. 'Come on, Patchie! That nasty cat won't get you again!'

When Buster stopped running, he sat in the sun and groomed the dog food crumbs off his face. Then, keeping close to bushes and shadowy trees, he started off in the direction of his home.

CHAPTER 7

It took Buster another two days to find his way back to Mr Larsen's house. Big dogs chased him and people shouted at him. Cars screeched to a stop when he raced across roads without looking. He tried to steal meat from a big dog, but an even bigger dog came out from its kennel, and both dogs were so angry they jumped the fence to chase him.

That was the only time Buster was really afraid, because he could chase two little dogs or one big dog, but he couldn't fight off two big dogs. It took a long rest behind a stack of firewood, and nearly ten minutes of extra grooming, before he was ready to start finding his way home again after that.

But an hour later he found half a meat pie on a picnic table, and that was so good he forgot all about being afraid.

Late that night, when he'd walked as far as he could for one day, he sneaked in a cat door to eat a huge bowl of dry food before chasing a fluffy white cat out of her comfy bed.

'Be quiet, Princess!' a man shouted down the stairs.

The white cat slunk off to hide behind the couch while Buster settled into her basket. He slept happily till the first rays of morning sun shone in the window. Then he slipped out the cat door before anyone was awake.

Finally, early on Saturday morning, he reached his home. He arched his back, rubbing happily against the front door and mewing to be let in.

No one came to the door. Buster stalked around to the back door, but it was shut tight. The lounge room window that he'd broken had been fixed, and it was closed too. There was no way in.

Buster crept back more cautiously to the front

door. He sniffed at it, and this time he didn't rub against it. He knew that Mr Larsen wasn't inside.

The big cat felt again the terror of Mr Larsen lying on the floor, the sirens, and people with metal trolleys taking his man away. He flattened his ears and crept under a bush to wait.

A car pulled into the driveway, and Buster watched Mr Larsen's son get out. He didn't move when the man went into the house and came out again with a tin of cat food.

'Here, Buster!' Mr Larsen's son called, waving the tin as he walked around the garden. 'Come on, puss!'

Buster was hungry, but he didn't like Mr Larsen's son, because whenever he visited, Buster wasn't allowed to sit near Mr Larsen. If the men sat inside, Buster had to go out, and if they sat on the verandah, Buster was shut inside.

So he waited while Mr Larsen's son walked right past the bush where he was hiding. He didn't even twitch when the man sneezed right in front of him.

The problem was that Mr Larsen's son hadn't ever spent any time with cats. He thought that waving a cat-food tin would be enough to make a frightened cat run out to meet him with a *thank you!* meow. Then he could go to the hospital and tell Mr Larsen he didn't need to worry anymore.

But Buster wasn't going to go to anyone except his own Mr Larsen.

CHAPTER 8

Josh dreamed that Buster was stuck in a rabbit hole. He knew that he had to pull him out, but then he turned into Buster, and there was no one anywhere to help. The more he thrashed and wriggled the more stuck he got, but he couldn't stop. Panic was rising in his throat; he was choking; he was never going to get out of here...

He woke up sweating, tangled in his sheet, with his heart thumping. *He's not even my cat!* he thought. *Why do I have to have nightmares about him?*

But by the time he got out of bed, he knew there was only one way to stop the gnawing ache inside him.

'Can we look for Buster again today?' he asked at breakfast.

'It won't be easy,' said his dad. 'Remember how good Rex was at hiding?'

Two years ago, in a lightning-flashing, window-rattling thunderstorm, Rex had disappeared. They'd searched every room, under every bed, behind the couch and in every corner, and they'd all felt sick worrying that somehow the rabbit had hopped out alone into the stormy night.

Josh remembered the birthday-party feeling of seeing Rex hop into the kitchen for breakfast the next morning, as if nothing had happened. He wanted that feeling again.

'We should check at Rainbow Street first,' said his mum. 'They might have found him already.'

They dropped Mai off at netball practice, and then Mr and Mrs Lee and Josh drove to Rainbow Street.

They walked down the path towards the cherry-coloured door. An old man was cleaning out a water trough, while three goats grazed under a tree. One goat had only three legs.

'That's horrible!' Josh said, pointing.

The goat looked up and walked away.

'Bessy doesn't like to be pointed at,' said Bert. 'But she does just fine with three legs now.'

They went inside.

'Can I help you?' someone asked.

Josh looked around. It sounded like the old man, but the only person in the room was Mona.

'You're not crazy,' Mona said. 'Gulliver sounds exactly like Bert. He thinks he's the receptionist.'

Josh started to laugh. It was the funniest thing he'd ever heard: a cockatoo that sounded like an old man and thought he was a receptionist. And when Josh laughed, Gulliver did too. He didn't laugh like an old man: he giggled like a little girl.

Then everyone was laughing. It was impossible not to, with Gulliver giggling and Josh spluttering. He hadn't laughed since Rex had died, and now Josh couldn't stop. He laughed till he was gasping for breath. His stomach ached and tears rolled down his face.

Bert came in to see what was happening.

'G'day, mate!' said the bird, and that started Josh all over again.

'Now,' said Mona, 'I'm guessing you didn't come just to see Gulliver?'

'We live near Mr Larsen,' said Mrs Lec. 'We've come to ask about Buster.'

'The cat with attitude, we called him,' said Mona. 'I just hope that attitude is helping him survive now.'

'Where do you think he could have gone?' asked Josh.

'He's most likely hiding somewhere near his house, or trying to get back to it,' said Mona. 'But a frightened animal can run a long way.'

'So he could be anywhere?' asked Mr Lee.

Mona nodded. 'And wherever he is, he can't live outside on his own. It's not safe for him, and it's not safe for any birds or possums he meets. We need to find him.'

Josh felt a lump of fear in his stomach, just like when he'd thought Rex had disappeared into the thunderstorm.

The next day was 'First Monday of the Month' assembly.

Josh had stayed up late working with his dad

to get ready for it, and he left for school early. He turned right at the first corner, and when he got to Mr Larsen's house, he opened the gate.

He knocked on the door just in case someone was there. No one was. Josh walked all around the outside of the house, peering into every corner of the garden.

'Here, Buster!' he called. 'Puss, puss, puss!'

There was no sign of a cat anywhere; not the faintest meow.

Josh walked slowly back down the footpath. His shoulders drooped and he scuffed his feet. He didn't want to go to school.

He stared through the fence of the house that was being built next door, but the garden had been bulldozed. There were just piles of wood, metal tubes and pipes – no bushy shrubs for a cat to crawl under, or leafy trees to climb.

Josh straightened up his backpack, and walked on to school.

I could still change my mind, he told himself, as he turned onto Ocean Street.

I don't have to do it, he thought as he waited for the crossing guard.

Why am I even thinking of doing it? he wondered as he walked in the gate.

'Because Buster's a lot more scared than I am,' he said aloud, as he stepped into the school hall.

He knew he had to do it.

Mrs Stevens was talking to the kids who were presenting this morning. Hannah was the last in line. Josh remembered how he'd wished he didn't have to listen to her talk about the pets in Rainbow Street. Now he wished that Buster was in the shelter too.

He took a deep breath and marched up to the principal.

It was the longest assembly Josh had ever sat through. There were announcements from teachers and reports from class captains, two girls singing a duet, and a boy playing a violin solo.

Then Hannah stepped up and told them about a dog that had arrived at the shelter last week and was ready to adopt.

'He's friendly and very, very cute,' said Hannah, showing a picture of a shaggy grey-and-white dog peeking out from beneath its woolly fringe.

'Awww,' breathed the audience.

Josh hoped they'd care as much about an ugly orange cat.

'And now,' said Mrs Stevens, 'we have one more urgent item.'

Josh walked across the stage. He could hardly breathe, and he felt as if he might throw up. He really, really didn't want to do that.

The microphone was too high; he was a lot shorter than Hannah. He heard someone laughing as he struggled to bend it down.

You can't run away now! Josh told himself.

He showed his first picture: a picture he'd found online of a big orange cat, with a big heading that read LOST CAT: BUSTER.

'Except Buster is a lot bigger,' said Josh. 'And he's got enormous paws.'

His voice squeaked as he said 'enormous' and the word echoed shrilly through the hall.

'To catch squeaky mice?' said the school bully.

'For a pipsqueak!' said someone else, and a wave of laughter rippled through the boys in the front row.

'That'll do!' said Mrs Stevens. 'Josh has something serious to tell us.'

Josh moved quickly to the headline from the newspaper article: CAT SAVES OWNER'S LIFE!

Finally he showed two phone numbers: the Lees', and the Rainbow Street Shelter's.

'Buster's not an ordinary cat,' Josh finished desperately. 'He's a hero. So if you've seen him, please tell me or take him to the animal shelter.'

His knees were wobbling as he walked back across the stage. Hannah smiled.

'You're not going to throw up, are you?' she whispered.

Josh's face glowed red as a traffic light. 'How did you know?'

'How do you think?' she asked. 'I always feel the same way.'

'Well, I'm not doing it again!' said Josh.

Lachlan caught up to him as they crowded into their classroom.

'I'd never have had the guts to stand up in assembly when I lost my dog. I really hope you find Buster.'

'Me too,' said Josh.

All the rest of the day, some kids made squeaky mouse noises when they saw Josh – but others came up and said that they had a cat too, or they had a pet who'd got lost once, and that they'd look for Buster on their way home. Even kids who didn't have a pet stopped and said, 'I hope you find your cat.'

But the next day, no one had seen a cat that could possibly be Buster.

CHAPTER 9

After school on Tuesday, Josh and his mum went back to the Rainbow Street Shelter – but Buster hadn't turned up there either.

'We can try putting a cage-trap at his house,' said Mona. 'I phoned Mr Larsen's son, and he said that would be okay.'

'Won't Buster hate being trapped?' Josh asked.

'Probably,' said Mona. 'The poor thing's been through plenty already, but a night in a cage is better than being hit by a car.'

Josh felt cold right through. He had to find him!

They carried the cage out to the car, went back

home for a tin of tuna and an old beach towel, and drove around to Mr Larsen's house. Josh felt like a burglar, sneaking up to someone's verandah knowing they weren't home.

'We're doing the right thing,' his mum said, but she knocked on the door first, just like Josh had the day before.

They opened the tuna and walked all around the garden again, brushing branches aside, peeking under bushes and calling, 'Here, Buster! Puss, puss, puss!'

But there wasn't a shadow of a cat, or an echo of a meow.

'We'll have to give up now,' said Mrs Lee. 'There's nothing more we can do.'

'I'll just check here first!' said Josh, because there was one more big bush that he hadn't crawled under. He was suddenly so sure Buster would be there that he could almost feel the cat's fur under his hands.

But Buster wasn't there either.

Josh thought about what Mona had said, and helped his mum put the cage on the verandah where Buster used to sit with Mr Larsen. He half-crawled in to lay the beach towel out, smooth and comfy for Buster to lie on. Then they put the open tin of tuna inside.

Once Buster went in to eat it, the door would close and he'd be safe till morning.

Josh woke up in the middle of the night and lay in the darkness for a long time, wondering whether Buster had found the tin of tuna.

All the while that Mrs Lee and Josh had been walking around the garden, Buster had flattened himself under a bush so low no one would think an enormous cat could possibly fit under it. He'd smelled the tuna, but after those days of being chased and afraid, he was not going to come out for anyone.

When they'd left, he could still smell the fish. All evening, the scent of tuna wafted towards him like a song. As soon as it was dark, Buster crept towards it.

He stretched one paw into the cage, as far as

he could, and batted the tin. It rolled a little bit closer. Buster wanted that tuna very badly; he whacked the tin harder. It bounced against the cage wall and rolled to the other end.

No matter what Buster did, he could not get it out. And no matter how badly he wanted it, he would not walk into that cage. Buster licked the taste of tuna off his claws, and stalked into the night.

So when Mrs Lee and Josh walked around to Mr Larsen's the next morning, the tuna tin was upside down at the end of the cage, the towel was scruffed up at the front, and Buster was nowhere to be seen.

For a minute Josh felt as empty as the cage.

'We can put a fresh tin of tuna in tonight,' said his mum.

But even as Josh straightened the towel and the overturned tin, part of him was glad that brave, crazy cat was free.

After Josh and Mrs Lee had gone, Buster came home, and slipped back up onto the verandah.

Buster had barely eaten since he'd got back to his house, and he was getting tired. It was hard work sneaking bits of food – and it was warm and peaceful on the verandah in the morning sun. He curled up on Mr Larsen's chair and fell fast asleep – so sound asleep that he didn't hear a man coming up the path.

'Hey, puss!' the man said, and patted Buster on the head.

Buster opened his eyes and saw a man with an orange cap leaning over him. With a wild yowl, he streaked off the verandah, his ears flat against his skull.

The man liked cats, and most cats liked him – so when he saw a cat as afraid as Buster, he knew there was something wrong.

'Here, puss!' he called. 'Puss, puss, puss!' He hunted all around the garden. 'There you are!' he said at last.

Buster was crouched in a corner behind the garage. His tail lashed and he hissed as the man came near.

'It's okay, mate,' the man said. He was sure that Buster was a stray that needed help. *If nobody claims him,* he thought, *I'll keep him.* He walked up slowly – then lunged at the frightened cat. Buster flew straight up the fence and over the other side, disappearing into the piles of building materials next door. The man shrugged, and went back to his job of hammering a big sign onto Mr Larsen's front lawn.

What if Buster's not hiding at his own place? Josh thought as he walked home from school. *He might have run miles away!*

He looked through the fence at the building site, but it didn't look like a place for a cat to hide.

Then Josh heard something.

'Meow.'

It was very faint. It sounded far away, and it

didn't sound tough enough to be a giant cat with attitude.

'Buster?' Josh called, walking back and forth beside the fence. 'Buster?'

'Meow,' the cat called back.

It still sounded faint, and it sounded scared.

Josh raced back to Mr Larsen's garden and looked behind the garage. 'Buster?' he called again.

He couldn't hear the mewing at all now, but there were scuff marks in the dirt and a tuft of orange cat hair on the fence. Buster had been there.

Josh dragged Mr Larsen's chair off the verandah and around to the back corner. Standing on the chair, he could pull himself up to the top of the fence. He swung his leg over and jumped down into the building site. He landed on his hands and feet, brushed the dirt off his hands, and called again.

'Buster?'

The mewing started again. It was coming from the pile of aluminium air-conditioning pipes.

CHAPTER 10

osh raced over to the stack of pipes. He crawled all around them, peering into each one, but he couldn't see a cat. He tried to lift one, but it was much too heavy. He hoped Buster wasn't trapped under them!

Josh put his foot on the top pipe and tried to roll it off. It rocked back and forth.

'MEOW!'

The sound was coming from deep inside the bottom pipe, which was bent like an elbow. It sounded as if Buster had got himself around that bend and didn't know how to get back. Josh raced around to the other end. There was a grid across it.

Josh wished he were so big and strong that he could just pick up the pipe and gently slide Buster out to safety. But he wasn't big and strong. He was small and skinny.

A little voice in Josh's head said he should go home and get help. But he wriggled into the pipe after the cat.

It was like crawling through the play-gym tunnel when he was in kindergarten, except that it was a lot narrower. The play-gym tunnel had been tall enough for little kids to crawl through on their hands and knees, but in this pipe there wasn't even room for Josh to spread his elbows to pull himself along: the only way was to slither like a snake, the metal ridges of the pipe pressing cold and hard against his stomach.

It was a lot darker than the play-gym tunnel too. And this pipe had a giant terrified cat stuck around the bend.

Josh was at the bend in the pipe. Now that he'd nearly reached Buster he remembered all the things he should have thought of first: like a tin of tuna, or a towel to wrap him in.

He wiggled his head and shoulders around the bend. He could just see the cat's shape as Buster backed up further, flattening himself against the grid at the end.

'Hi Buster,' said Josh. 'It's me.'

Buster mewed. It was the little kitten mew that Josh had heard from the outside.

'It's okay,' Josh told him. 'I'm going to get you out of here.'

Very, very slowly, he reached towards the cat. 'Mr Larsen wouldn't like you to be stuck in here, would he?' he said. He knew that Buster didn't understand what he was saying, but he had to keep on trying. 'Mr Larsen says you're a hero. He wants you to come out and have some tuna.'

Buster pushed his head against Josh's hand and let Josh stroke him gently over his head and down his neck, which was as far as Josh could reach.

'You ready to go back now?' Josh asked.

Buster didn't move.

Josh wriggled in a bit further. Now he could reach right around the cat, but he kept his face down against the metal floor. If he was going to get scratched, the top of his head was better than his face.

'This is probably the dumbest thing I've ever done,' he told Buster.

With his arm around the cat's back, he pulled Buster gently towards him. Buster didn't scratch or fight, but he didn't help either; he just let Josh pull him, as if he was too tired to care what happened.

It's not easy inching backwards around a bend in a tight metal tunnel, but it's even harder when you're pulling a cat that doesn't want to move. For a minute Josh remembered his nightmare and thought he wasn't going to be able to do it. He knew he should have gone home and asked for help instead of crawling in here all alone.

But all he could do was slide slowly backwards, coaxing the cat and pulling him, inch by inch.

He eased his shoulders back around the bend, then his head. Then slowly, slowly, he tugged Buster back down the tunnel.

It seemed a long way, even further than it had been going in. Josh didn't know how long he'd been in the pipe, and he couldn't guess how much further he had to go.

His left foot touched dirt.

Josh paused. He was nearly there – but he was going to have to hold on tight to Buster. He couldn't lose the cat just as they burst free of the pipe!

He was concentrating so hard it took a minute to hear the voice from outside. 'Josh! Josh – are you in there?'

'I've got Buster,' he called. 'He's really scared.'

'So was I!' snapped his mum.

Josh was finally out. He stood up with Buster in his arms.

His mum's face was white and tense. Behind her were two construction workers.

'When I found your bag behind the fence, I phoned the number on the gate here,' she said. 'These men came and let me in.'

'There's a reason it's locked,' the taller man said. 'We don't want kids getting hurt going places they're not supposed to be.'

'Sorry,' said Josh.

'Lucky you're so skinny,' said the other man.

'If you'd got stuck in that pipe you'd have been in real trouble!'

Josh carried Buster to where Mrs Lee had parked, in front of Mr Larsen's house. Buster was heavy, but Josh liked carrying him, and Buster seemed to think that was okay.

There was a sign on the front lawn.

FOR SALE.

CHAPTER 11

osh's mum didn't know which hospital Mr Larsen was in, so she tried to phone his son in Sydney. There was no answer.

'Let's go and get Buster checked out,' she said, 'and then we'll be able to give Mr Larsen the good news.'

Mona had told them that Buster didn't like going in cars, so Mrs Lee got the beach towel from the cage. She wrapped it around the frightened cat before settling him into Josh's arms.

And maybe it was because she drove to Rainbow Street so slowly and carefully, or maybe because he knew that Josh had saved him, Buster didn't panic at all.

Mona was waiting for them at the gate. 'Hey, Hero Cat,' she said softly, leaning in to stroke the furry orange head.

Buster rubbed against her hand and meowed, sounding a little more like himself now.

'And Hero Boy,' Mona added.

Josh blushed.

'I guess your mum's already told you what a stupid thing you did – so I'll just say thanks.'

She clipped a leash onto Buster's collar and gave the other end to Josh. 'For most cats, it's a carry-case,' she said. 'But Buster's not most cats!'

Josh and Buster walked up the path. Buster was almost swaggering again by the time they got into the vet's examination room.

The vet checked inside Buster's mouth and ears, felt all over his body for cuts and scratches, took his temperature and listened to his heart. 'He's hungry and tired, and still a bit shocked,' she said. 'But he's going to be absolutely fine.'

'There is a problem though,' Mona said, and her eyes filled up with tears.

Josh held his breath.

'Buster's okay, but Mr Larsen isn't,' she said. 'The doctors have told him that his hip is never going to be strong enough for him to live alone again, and he's going to move in with his son.'

'But his son's in Sydney!' said Mrs Lee.

'Yes,' said Mona. 'But the real problem is that his son is allergic to cats. Mr Larsen can't take Buster with him.'

Josh felt his breath catch in his throat. 'What's going to happen to Buster?'

'Mr Larsen asked if we could find him a new home.'

'No!' shouted Josh. 'We can't leave him here again!'

Mrs Lee had already pulled out her phone. 'Meet us at the Rainbow Street Shelter,' she told Mr Lee and Mai. 'It's urgent!'

'Have you really thought about this?' Mona asked, when the whole family was there. 'When we talked before, you said Mrs Lee wanted a bunny and Mai wanted a dog.'

'I never wanted a pet again,' admitted Josh.

'But now you're choosing a cat?' said Mona.

'Not just any cat!' they all said. 'It's Buster.'

Mona smiled. 'Sometimes that happens,' she said. 'Sometimes life chooses a pet for you.'

CHAPTER 12

At first Buster only liked doing the things that he used to do with Mr Larsen. He liked going for a walk at the beach every afternoon, and sitting on the deck with them when they had dinner outside.

Mrs Lee bought him a catnip mouse, and Josh made a fishing pole to dangle feathers in front of his enormous paws, but Buster just looked at the toys as if he'd never heard of play.

He never tried to run away, but one afternoon when Josh was walking him on his leash, Buster turned to go up the street past Mr Larsen's old house.

'You don't live there anymore,' Josh reminded him.

But Buster sat down on the footpath and wouldn't move till Josh walked up the street.

A young woman was sitting on the verandah where Mr Larsen used to sit, watching her little twins playing in a new sandpit.

She smiled when she saw Josh and his enormous orange cat walking on a leash.

'That's the biggest cat I've ever seen!' she called. 'What's his name?'

'Buster,' said Josh.

Buster quivered, and walked on.

That night, when Mrs Lee was making dinner, she accidentally dropped a long, curling carrot peel on the floor. Buster leapt and caught it, then threw and chased it all around the living room till he lost it behind the couch cushions. He couldn't get his paw down the back of the couch. He mewed loudly for someone to find it for him.

Mr and Mrs Lee, Mai and Josh all came running. Mr Lee pulled out the broken carrot peel, and Mrs Lee peeled a new one. She tossed it on the floor – and Buster leapt after it.

When that carrot peel was too broken to throw,

Josh got out the fishing-pole toy. He trailed the feather in front of Buster, and the big cat pounced. Josh flicked it high, and Buster leapt high. They played round and round the room, trailing and pouncing, flicking and leaping.

By the time Josh's favorite program came on, Buster had shredded the feather and torn it right off the fishing-pole string. Josh got a piece of paper and crumpled it into a tight ball. He sat down on the couch so he could watch the TV while he tied the paper ball to the end of the string.

Buster bounded across the room and poured himself onto Josh's lap. As he settled in, the cat began to purr. It started off as a whispery hum, but as the boy's hands stroked the thick fur from the top of his head, down his back to the start of his tail, Buster's purr rumbled louder and louder. After a few minutes his whole body thrummed like a fishing boat heading out to sea.

Dear Josh,

Thank you for your letter and pictures of Buster - and thank you again, from the bottom of my heart, for searching for him, and for your bravery in rescuing him once you found him. Asking the folks at Rainbow Street to find Buster a new home was the hardest thing I've ever done, and it makes me very happy to know he's settled in with you.

I'm sending you a picture too, because last week my son and his wife brought home a little dog from the animal shelter here. It's a mostly poodle, so my son is not allergic to it.

I didn't think I ever wanted to get to know another animal, but this fellow didn't give me a choice. Buster will always have his own space in my heart, but it seems there's room for a little dog as well.

Thank you for finding space for Buster in your heart, and your home.

Yours truly,

Edward Larsen

STOLEN!

A Pony Called Pebbles

CHAPTER 1

The stables on the hill were shadowed and quiet in the moonlight. As the two men in dark clothes crept down the long hall, they could smell the warm scent of clean horses and fresh hay.

'Go right to the end,' the leader hissed.

They snuck into the last stall, where Pebbles was sleeping. She was short and stocky, silvery-white with darker grey dapples across her rump. Her eyes were soft and brown in her pretty face.

'That's not a racehorse!' the smaller thief snarled. 'We're in the wrong stall!'

A tall black stallion sprang to his feet. The men heard his hooves strike the floor. They felt the rush of his powerful body, and now that their eyes were used to the darkness, they saw his shape.

'*That's* Midnight!' the leader exclaimed.

Before the stallion knew what was happening, a rope was around his neck and looped over his nose into a halter.

The horse's eyes rolled white with fear and rage. He jerked back and reared, his strong front legs slashing the air. The man holding the halter was thrown into the corner of the stall. He rolled out of the way just as Midnight's hooves thudded down.

'Forget it!' the other man screamed. 'I'm not getting killed just to steal a horse!'

'Be quiet!' said the boss thief. He opened the stall door and pushed the smaller man out to the hall.

The stallion pawed the floor, snorting in alarm.

The thief ignored him. He rubbed the silver mare between her ears and breathed gently into her nostrils.

'What are you doing?' said the other man. 'That's not the one we want!'

'I'm guessing that big devil doesn't go anywhere

without his little friend. And when you're worth as much as he is, what you want, you get.'

The thief slipped a rope halter over Pebbles' head too.

CHAPTER 2

Ellie had wanted a horse for as long as she could remember. She liked ponies, but what she really wanted was a horse. She drew horses, painted horses, collected horse books, horse ornaments and pictures, and watched horse DVDs. She wanted one so badly that sometimes she pretended that she *was* a horse. When she ran barefoot on the lawn, she imagined that her feet were hooves striking the ground. She practised trotting with her knees high, and cantering fast and smooth, with her left leg leading.

Other times she pretended that her bike was a horse, even though she had to do the pedalling.

But mostly she just imagined what it would

be like to have her own horse. She would brush its big body and comb its long mane. She would look into its eyes and climb on its back, and ride it everywhere.

'Ellie,' her mum always said, 'you know we can't have a horse! Horses are expensive – and where would we keep it?'

Hannah had been Ellie's best friend since kindergarten. They did so many things together that Ellie's dad called them the Ellie–Hannah twins, even though they didn't look the same. Ellie's hair was black, short and shiny, while Hannah had a thick brown ponytail that bounced when she was happy, and drooped when she was sad.

The other difference was that even though Ellie loved horses as much as Hannah loved dogs, Hannah had her own dog now.

Just like Ellie's parents, Hannah's parents always used to say there was no way they could have a dog. But when Hannah became a volunteer at the Rainbow Street Shelter and helped look after a mother dog with five new puppies, Mr and Mrs Cooper said she could keep one. So Hannah took home the brown-and-white puppy she called Peanut – and her mum adopted his shaggy white mother.

And even though she had Peanut now, Hannah still went to the shelter every Saturday to help Mona and Bert clean out the runs and play with the dogs that were waiting for new homes. Tonight Ellie was sleeping over, so she was going to Rainbow Street in the morning too.

In the horse float behind the truck, the tall black stallion and the silver mare stamped nervously.

The two thieves in the truck were even more nervous. They'd planned to drive all night and be far away by morning. But it had taken so long to load Midnight into the float that now it was nearly daylight. Soon people would be arriving at the stables to feed and exercise the horses. They'd see that the last stall was empty and call the police.

'We've got to get off this road,' the leader muttered. 'There's no way I'm going back to jail!'

But the road from the stables ran along beside

the bush, and so far they hadn't seen any side roads leading off it. They drove faster. The horses in the float whinnied as they were bumped and jolted. Finally, just as the sun came up, the truck slowed at a sign with picnic tables.

'Are you crazy?' the other thief shouted. 'We can't stop for a picnic – the police will see the float and catch us for sure!'

'Not if we don't have any horses with us,' said the driver. He turned into the entrance to the park.

The horses felt the float stop. Branches crowded against the blackened windows so no light came through at all. No one came to get them out, or even to rub their noses and talk to them.

The stallion whinnied, and the white mare nickered quietly back. '*Don't worry*,' she seemed to say, '*I'm here. We'll be okay together.*'

She wouldn't have been so sure if she could have seen the two thieves. They were working as fast as they could, hauling wire and fencing tools from the truck deep into the bush.

At the top of a rocky ravine they stopped. 'Perfect!' said the leader, pointing down to the creek. 'If they've got water, they'll survive till we come back.'

'There's not much for them to eat,' said the smaller man.

The boss thief laughed a nasty sort of laugh. 'The hungrier they are, the easier they'll be to catch.'

They began to string the wire through the trees to make a fence.

CHAPTER 3

he big black horse stamped so hard the whole float shuddered. Even Pebbles was getting twitchy: it was time for her breakfast. Any minute now someone should come with horse pellets for her and her friend. Usually it was a girl; other days it was a boy – but whoever it was would pat and brush her, check her feet and rub between her ears.

Midnight always snorted and skittered when the groom came into the big stall, but the mare liked being brushed. Even though she was so much smaller than the stallion, she would push in front of him. And the longer she stood, nodding her head in rhythm with the long strokes of the brush, the calmer Midnight became. By the time

Pebbles was shining, from her combed-out silvery mane to her round black hooves, the stallion was ready to be groomed too.

Finally they would both be saddled and bridled. Midnight would begin to quiver again, but his companion would lead him calmly outside. Their riders would mount, and they would canter together around the track.

Sometimes the mare would go around the track two or three times; sometimes she was only halfway around when her rider reined her in. Wherever it was, Pebbles gradually dropped back till she could trot out the next gate. Then she and her rider would watch from the railings as her big black friend burst from a canter to a gallop. Faster and faster he'd go, his hooves thundering on the hard ground, his long legs flashing in a blur.

When he finally pulled up, his nostrils flaring red and shoulders lathered with sweat, no matter how much his rider stroked and soothed him, all that Midnight wanted was to see the silver mare. Only when she was standing beside him could he relax and enjoy the trainer's praise.

But now it was full daylight. They were still in

the horse float, and still hadn't had their breakfast. Midnight tossed his head and tried to rear, but was jerked back hard by the short rope tying him to the bar. The silver mare quivered. She was tied too tight to reach over and nuzzle her friend, and now she was anxious too. She neighed impatiently when she heard the men return.

'Get the mare out first,' she heard one of them say.

The smaller thief untied the end of Pebbles' rope and tugged her backwards out of the float. She stepped down cautiously and looked around. She'd never been in such dark dense bush before.

The leader stepped into the empty side of the float and untied the stallion's rope.

'Take her ahead—' he called, but before he could finish the sentence, Midnight shot out of the float as if he was on springs. The thief bounced behind him on the end of the rope. He yanked the stallion's head hard.

The other man was already leading the white horse to the ravine. She nickered anxiously, and Midnight whinnied back as he followed her into the wire corral. But as soon as she was let go, Pebbles trotted off to explore this strange new place.

The big black horse reared, ripping the rope out of the thief's hands and galloping to her side.

'That's why we brought her,' he said. As fast as they could, the two men looped the wire around trees to close the opening in the fence. 'We'd have never got him in there without her.'

'What if he trips on that rope?'

'You try to get it off if you want – I'm not going in there with him again!'

The stallion trumpeted defiantly and the two men hurried back to the truck. They unhitched the float, shoving it as far as they could under a wide-spreading tree.

'Hurry up!' the leader growled, but the other man broke branches off bushy shrubs and heaped them up in front of the float, till it was nearly impossible to see from the road. Then he jumped into the truck too.

They sped out of the park and down the road.

Ten minutes later, they saw a police car racing towards them, lights flashing and siren wailing. It slowed for a moment as it came close, then sped on towards the stables. The two thieves laughed all the way to the highway.

CHAPTER 4

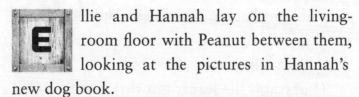llie and Hannah lay on the living-room floor with Peanut between them, looking at the pictures in Hannah's new dog book.

'You're the cutest,' Hannah told Peanut. The puppy rolled onto his back, waving his front paws as if he knew exactly what 'cute' meant.

Mrs Cooper sat down on the couch with Peanut's shaggy white mother on her lap. 'And Molly's the smartest, because she always watches the news with me!'

She flicked on the TV. On the screen, a tall black horse with a grinning jockey on his back skittered through a cheering crowd.

'Last year's winner of the Melbourne Cup, Master Midnight, was stolen from the Green Hills stables last night. The owner, Mrs Barrington, said that the stallion refuses to travel anywhere without his companion pony, Pebbles. The thieves apparently knew this, as Pebbles is also missing.'

Ellie wished there'd been a picture of the pony too. 'Pebbles' sounded just right for a round, shaggy Shetland. She'd have liked to see it together with that huge racehorse.

The two thieves were back in the park very early the next morning. While it was still dark, they pulled the branches away from the horse float, dragged it out from under the trees and hitched it to the tow bar.

The boss thief got a bucket and a scoopful of oats from the back of the truck.

'Let's hope they're hungry,' said the other man.

'I just hope they're still there!' said the leader.

In the soft predawn light, they followed the trail they'd used the day before, and pushed through the bush to the ravine. The horses were down at the creek, nosing for the blades of fresh grass that grew by the water. They were very hungry.

The men ducked through the wire gate. The leader swished the oats in the bucket. 'Breakfast!' he called, in the friendliest voice he could manage. 'Come and get it!'

Pebbles scrambled quickly up the hill.

Midnight hesitated, but when he saw his friend's head dip into the bucket, he neighed and charged after her.

The smaller man clipped a rope onto Pebbles' halter. The other grabbed the bucket away from her and swished the oats again to call the stallion. The mare struggled to get it back.

The big black horse stopped. His nostrils flared. He didn't like these men – but he knew that if Pebbles wanted what was in there, he did too. He stretched his neck out as far as he could and snatched a mouthful of oats.

The boss thief grabbed the rope dangling from his halter as the other man cut the wire gate open and led the white mare towards the horse float.

Pebbles was sure that she'd be fed as soon as she got into the float. She loaded quickly, and the big horse followed her. The boss thief tied the stallion's head tight. 'Now get the mare out!'

'Hang on,' said the smaller man. 'I've got a fool-proof plan!' He closed the float gate, and snipped off the long silvery hairs of the pony's tail with a pair of shears. Then he taped the grey tail on top of the stallion's black one. 'And now,' he said, 'let's make him white!' He took a spray can, and sprayed Midnight's back and neck until they were covered with white shaving foam. Then he backed Pebbles out of the float. The leader slammed the tailgate shut before the black horse could move.

'Now, what can you see?' the smaller thief asked.

The boss checked from behind the float, as if he were in a car following it. 'One *white* horse!'

'And everyone's looking for a black horse and a white pony!'

The two thieves high-fived triumphantly.

The stallion trumpeted angrily.

The mare neighed back, and refused to budge even when the men waved their arms at her and shouted.

Inside the float, Midnight thrashed and struggled. He tried to rear, and kicked the back door with his strong hind legs, but he was tied tight and the float was solid. He could not escape.

The boss thief clipped a rope onto the mare's halter. Tugging and yanking, he hauled her back through the trees to the corral, and didn't let her go till the other man had wired it shut again.

'We can pick her up later if that black devil doesn't settle down,' he said. 'Now let's get out of here!'

With Pebbles' grey tail floating behind the talegate, they disappeared down the road.

Peanut was supposed to sleep in his own basket, but as soon as the first rays of sun shone in the window, the puppy would always leap onto Hannah's bed, cover her face with kisses, and then snuggle down to sleep beside her till it was time to get up. This morning, since Ellie was in the spare bed, he bounced back and forth between the two of them.

Ellie thought it was a good way to wake up before going to the animal shelter.

'It's the best way to wake up *every* day,' said Hannah.

Pebbles raced back and forth along the fence at the top of the ravine, neighing desperately.

Her friend didn't come back. After a while she gave up and went back to searching for something green to eat. There hadn't been much grass to start with, and she and Midnight had eaten most of it the day before.

Hannah's dad dropped the girls off at the shelter right after breakfast. They needed to be there early that morning, because afterwards Hannah's family was driving up to the hills for a picnic. Ellie was going with them.

The little blue house was prettier than Ellie had imagined an animal shelter could be. She smiled as she stepped under the rainbow at the door.

Hannah tapped on the door, and they went in. A grey cat watched them from the windowsill.

'Can I help you?' squawked Gulliver, from his perch above the desk.

Ellie laughed.

Mona came in from the SMALL ANIMAL ROOM, with her little dog Nelly following close behind. 'Where would you like to help?' she asked Ellie.

'Are there any horses?' Ellie asked.

Mona shook her head. 'You never know what's going to turn up here next – but we haven't had a lost horse for ages.'

So Ellie took some hay out to Bessy, the three-legged goat, and checked that her water trough was full. Bert arrived and showed Ellie how to brush the goat's coat to get all the extra hair out and keep her skin healthy. Bessy liked being groomed. She leaned against Ellie as Ellie brushed, and rubbed her head against Ellie's back when she'd finished.

'She's saying thank you,' said Bert.

CHAPTER 5

olly and Peanut were in the car when the Coopers picked Ellie and Hannah up from Rainbow Street. 'They're part of the family!' Hannah's dad said. 'We couldn't go on a picnic without them!'

They drove along the coast for nearly half-an-hour before Mr Cooper turned onto the road into the hills. Hannah and Ellie were getting bored in the back seat. Peanut bounced between them, standing on Hannah's legs to look out the right-hand window, then on Ellie's to look out the left. He was very cute, but his claws were scratchy.

His shaggy mother sat quietly at Mrs Cooper's feet. Every few minutes she'd stroke the dog's ears, and Molly would look up adoringly at her.

Peanut adored Hannah, but he was too busy to stop and look at her.

'Nearly there!' said Hannah's dad, pointing ahead to a sign.

They kept on driving. Now the road wound along with the hills and bush on one side and farms on the other. Ellie looked out at the farms, hoping to see horses. So far all she'd seen were sheep.

The day would be perfect if she could just see a horse.

Pebbles had covered every bit of the bush where she was fenced in. She'd scrambled down to the creek to drink and nosed the rocks to see if any of them were hiding something to eat. There was no food anywhere.

Now she was going along the wire fence with her neck stretched out under the bottom strand to reach the last bits of grass on the other side. She wasn't a big horse, and didn't need nearly as much to eat as Midnight. But she was getting very hungry.

Hannah's dad followed the signs to a grassy clearing with picnic tables. The bush around them was thick and shady.

'Let's take the dogs for a walk before lunch,' said Hannah's mum.

Ellie was glad there were tracks to walk on. She'd be afraid to push her way through those trees. There might be snakes, giant spiders or other creepy insects waiting to drop into her hair...Peanut bounced on the end of his leash, but Molly walked politely, and Mrs Cooper let Ellie take her. The girls and the dogs ran ahead.

'Don't turn off to the lake – it's too far!' Hannah's dad shouted.

Up ahead they could see flashes of blue water through the trees where the path curved and split. The right-hand path led around the lake to where a creek flowed into it through a deep ravine. 'LAKE CIRCUIT WALK: 10 KILOMETRES,' said the sign.

'We can do it after lunch,' said Hannah's mum.

Ellie looked longingly at the lake trail. She didn't know why she wanted to go that way so badly – she just knew she did. But she turned around obediently and followed Hannah and her parents along the left-hand trail that looped back towards the car.

The picnic was fancy, with cold roast chicken, potato salad, coleslaw, carrot sticks, meatloaf, rolls, strawberries, peaches and a chocolate cake. It took a long time, and even when they were tidying up the plates and leftovers, and Ellie thought they were finally ready to go on the walk, Hannah's dad poured two more cups of coffee.

'To go!' he said, before Hannah could protest.

They started back down the trail, the girls with the dogs, and Hannah's parents with their coffees. This time, when they reached the lake, they turned right. Peanut and Molly sniffed the air happily, rushing from side to side to find smell-signposts in the bushes and see what other animals had crossed the path ahead of them.

Hannah's dad stopped at a wooden bench on a curve where the creek flowed into the lake. The trail continued on down beside the creek.

'We'll sit here and finish our coffees,' he said. 'Catch you up in a minute.'

'Don't go off the trail!' Hannah's mum called.

Hannah and Ellie raced ahead with the dogs; even quiet Molly was bouncing as much as her son.

'The air smells different here,' Ellie said.

Hannah took a big breath, tasting it. 'Wild air!'

They laughed, and ran on.

The creek running beside the trail was shallow and narrow. It was cut deep into the rocky banks, as if a long time ago it had been a bigger, wilder river. The girls came to a wooden bridge and gazed down into the ravine below. It was steeper and deeper than it seemed from the trail. The dogs sniffed the bridge cautiously.

'Come on!' Ellie coaxed shaggy Molly, and they galloped across the bridge, their feet thundering like horses' hooves. When they got to the path on the other side, the dogs raced ahead, relieved to be back on solid ground.

If she couldn't ride a horse, Ellie decided, the next best thing was pretending to be one, with a dog tugging at the leash like a horse at its reins.

'Hannah!' Hannah's dad shouted. 'Ellie!'

The girls looked around; they hadn't realised they'd run so far. They turned and ran back towards the bridge.

Hannah's parents were staring down at the creek. 'I heard something moving around in the bush – I thought maybe you'd gone down there and got lost!' said Hannah's mum.

'I told you they wouldn't go off the track,' said Mr Cooper.

Mrs Cooper was still looking down into the bush. 'I wonder what it was!'

'Can we go see?' asked Hannah.

'It's too steep,' her mum said quickly.

They walked back across the bridge, the dogs leading the way.

Pebbles could hear voices. Voices meant people … and people meant food. People could get her out of this place.

She charged to the top of the bank, whinnying loudly. She trotted back and forth through the trees along the fence, and whinnied again.

No one came.

'Did you hear that?' Ellie asked. 'It sounded like a horse!'

They were back on the trail around the lake. Everyone stopped and listened. Birds called and frogs croaked. No one could hear anything else.

'You've got horses on the brain,' Hannah teased.

They kept on going.

The thieves had been driving all day. Their old truck was hot and dusty, and they were hot and thirsty.

At lunchtime they pulled into a service station. 'Fill it fast!' said the boss thief, and the smaller man jumped out.

Midnight started kicking. He thrashed and reared till the whole float rocked, and a hoof-sized dent appeared in the tailgate. People filling their cars stared.

'Is that horse okay?' called a woman in riding boots, coming towards them.

The thief jumped back into the truck. 'The shaving cream's run off!' he hissed.

The driver swung back onto the highway so fast the tyres squealed. The float rattled behind, with Midnight still kicking and trumpeting.

'We'll take the back road,' he decided. 'We don't want anyone else looking at him.'

'Not till we get there!' said the smaller man, rubbing his hands together greedily.

The back road was twisty and narrow. There were no service stations. An hour later, the thieves were sweating and the truck was spluttering.

'What if we run out of petrol?' the smaller man asked nervously.

'We won't,' said the driver, slowing down to turn into a driveway with tall black gates. 'This is where we're going!'

The truck coughed, shuddered – and stopped in the middle of the road.

'Get out and push!' shouted the driver.

'Get the horse out yourself!' the smaller man shouted back.

They were shouting so loudly they didn't hear the police car till it was right behind them.

CHAPTER 6

M*aybe Hannah's right*, Ellie thought as she and the Coopers walked on. *Maybe I do just have horses on the brain. That's what Mum always says.*

The silver mare gave up whinnying and went on searching for food. She noticed a scrubby tree on the other side of the fence. It didn't look like anything she'd ever eaten before, but it was green and fresh. She stuck her head through the two middle wires and snatched a mouthful of leaves.

Her rope halter caught on a twist of wire. She

tugged, and the wire slipped further through the nose strap. The harder she tugged the tighter the wire got.

Pebbles was stuck tight with her head between the two wires of the fence.

The path took them right around the lake. Near the end, it forked again, with a shortcut leading straight back to the picnic site. The other arm looped back towards the creek and ended up where they'd begun.

'I know which way I'm going,' said Hannah's mum, turning onto the shortcut.

'But we wanted to do the ten k walk!' said Hannah.

Her dad laughed. 'Okay. Take the dogs and stay on the track. We'll meet you at the other end.'

The two girls grinned at each other. They both wanted to say that they'd walked ten kilometres. It hadn't been nearly as hard as it sounded.

'It's good walking with the dogs,' said Ellie.

'I knew you'd like it,' said Hannah.

Ten minutes later, when the end of the trail was nearly in sight, Ellie heard it again: a horse whinnying. Peanut barked, and Molly stopped, listening.

'That *did* sound like a horse,' Hannah admitted.

'But it sounds like it's back at the creek! Nobody would be riding there!'

They turned around and ran back towards the sound. Here, the trail ran along the top of the ravine for about a hundred metres. Ellie knew for sure they hadn't seen a horse when they'd walked along it a few minutes ago – and there definitely wasn't a horse there now.

'We'll have to go back,' said Hannah. 'Mum and Dad will be wondering where we are.'

Ellie nodded, and turned around with her friend. There was nothing else she could do. If they really had heard a horse, its rider would look after it. It didn't need her.

And then, just as they were nearly back at the end of the trail, Molly dashed into the bush, yanking her leash so hard she nearly pulled Ellie off her feet.

'Whoa!' Ellie shouted.

A horse neighed back. It was the strangest neigh Ellie had ever heard – but it definitely came from a horse. Ellie raced into the bush after the little dog. Hannah hesitated a moment, and followed.

Pebbles was normally calm and quiet, but she had been stuck with her head through the wire for nearly an hour. The more she struggled, the tighter the rope strap pulled, and the tighter it pulled, the more panicky she got. By the time Ellie burst through the trees, the horse's ears were laid back flat with fear, and her silvery shoulders were covered with sweat.

The dogs barked frantically. Ellie pulled Molly back.

'It's okay, horse,' she said, trying to keep her voice low and comforting. 'I'll help you.'

'I'll get Dad!' Hannah called. 'He can cut the wire!'

'Take the dogs!' Ellie said. 'They're scaring it.'

Hannah grabbed both leashes and raced back through the trees.

Ellie came closer. Of all the horse books she'd

read and DVDs she'd watched, none of them had ever told her how to untangle a horse with its halter caught through a wire.

But the horse couldn't wait for Hannah's parents. Ellie had to do something now.

The wire hook was poking through the side of the noseband. A smear of red blood stained the horse's silvery muzzle, where the wire and rope had rubbed the skin raw.

Ellie tried everything she could think of. She tried to pull the rope band off the wire; tried to straighten out the wire; tried to undo the halter's rope knot. Nothing worked. The wire was too strong, and the rope was pulled too tight. Her fingers couldn't even loosen the knot. Ellie's eyes filled with tears as the mare pulled back again, yanking the halter tighter on her head.

'NO!' Ellie said desperately. 'Bring your head forward!'

The terrified horse rolled her eyes.

Ellie put her arms around the big grey head and tried to pull it forward. The mare was too panicked now to know that she was being helped. She pulled back harder.

'Come on,' Ellie coaxed. She was still trying to sound calm, but her voice was squeaky and her hands were trembling. Angrily, she brushed her tears away. She was never going to be able to help this horse if she kept on crying.

But she knew she wasn't strong enough to pull the horse's head forward and down, the way it needed to go. Not from the ground.

Ellie looked towards the track, but there was no sign of Hannah and her parents. 'You've got to trust me, horse!' she said.

The horse's back was higher than Ellie's head, but the ground was steep. Ellie stood on a rock and grabbed the silvery mane with both hands.

The first time she tried to jump, she was standing too far away, and she just fell off the rock without touching the horse. She tried again, landed against the horse's side, and slipped back off.

But I've got to do it! she thought. *Nothing else is going to work.*

She grabbed the mane again, jumped, pulled herself up...and landed across the horse's back, with her head on one side and her feet on the other.

At the back of her mind, Ellie was surprised

that she could do this – but she didn't have time to think. She threw her right leg over the horse's rump, and sat up as if she was ready to ride.

The mare didn't seem to notice. She was still yanking back at the fence.

'Come on, Silvie,' Ellie said. She'd thought she was going to say 'Silver', but when it came out, Silvie seemed like a better name for such a pretty horse. She squeezed her legs against the round white sides the way riders did in horse books.

Silvie didn't move. Ellie squeezed again, harder, and clucked the way a horse-whisperer did in a program she'd watched.

The horse swayed, as if she was thinking about moving.

Ellie leaned forward, sliding all her weight onto Silvie's head, pushing it down as hard as she could. The horse took one step towards the fence, shifting her head just a few centimetres further out and down.

The halter unhooked itself from the wire.

Ellie slid down the smooth silvery neck and tumbled onto the ground just as Hannah and her parents rushed up to the corral.

CHAPTER 7

annah's mum was mostly worried about whether Ellie was okay.

Hannah's dad was wondering how and why the horse was there.

Hannah couldn't believe that her horse-crazy friend had not only found a horse, but had rescued it.

Ellie was full of the warm smell of horse, and so jumbled with emotions that she didn't know what she thought.

She wanted to laugh because Silvie was nuzzling her face, as if she was checking that Ellie was okay, and she'd never known that a horse's lips would be so rubbery and tickly. She was glowing with happiness because Silvie liked her. She was just about bursting in amazement that she'd got onto a horse all by herself, even if she had fallen off in three seconds. She was sad about the cut on Silvie's face, and angry when she noticed that her tail had been chopped off so that she couldn't swish away flies.

But most of all, Ellie was worried about what they were going to do with Silvie now that she was free. 'We can't just leave her here!' she said.

'She must belong to somebody,' said Hannah's mum. 'We can't steal a horse.'

'But there's no grass for her to eat!' Ellie protested. 'And what if she gets stuck again?'

'There's definitely something strange going on,' said Hannah's dad. 'But I don't know what we can do about it.'

'We could phone Mona,' said Hannah.

'I'll meet you there,' said Mona.

While they waited, Ellie used Mrs Cooper's phone to call her parents. At first her mother thought she was joking when Ellie said she'd found a horse.

'She really did!' Hannah's mum said.

'Rescued it!' said Hannah's dad.

'I'm very proud of you, Ellie,' her mum said. 'And I wish I could say that you could keep it. But even if they can't find out who it belongs to, there's absolutely no way we can have a horse.'

'I know,' Ellie whispered, even though deep down she'd been wishing that she could keep it. She gave the phone back to Hannah's mum and went on patting the horse's face. Silvie was busy checking the ground for any blade of grass she might have missed, but she didn't mind Ellie patting her at the same time.

Ellie wished she had something for her to eat. 'When I was little,' she told Hannah, 'I always used to put a carrot in my pocket, just in case I met a horse.'

Hannah laughed. 'I used to stuff biscuits in my pockets in case I met a dog.'

'So that's why dogs always followed you!' exclaimed her dad.

'We've got carrot sticks left from the picnic,' said her mum. 'The horse can have those.'

Ellie could hardly bear to leave for a minute, but she knew Silvie needed food more than pats.

'I'll go with you,' said Hannah's mum.

They pushed their way back through the trees to the trail. Mrs Cooper was walking so fast Ellie had to jog to keep up. 'I don't like leaving the dogs alone in the car,' she explained.

'I wonder how long that poor horse has been all alone!' Ellie burst out.

Hannah's mum hugged her. 'What matters is that you found it. It'll be all right now.'

Ellie hoped she was right.

Six leftover carrot sticks didn't seem very much to feed a horse. There was some chocolate cake left too, but Mrs Cooper said it was better to wait for Mona than to feed the horse something that might make it sick.

'I'll pick her some grass too,' Ellie decided, because the grass around the picnic site was thick, green and exactly what horses liked. She picked handfuls of grass into a shopping bag. It was going to take a long time to fill.

'If we had a leash we could bring the horse up here to eat,' she said.

'A dog leash wouldn't be strong enough,' said

Hannah's mum, but she opened the car boot and started rummaging. 'Here you go!' she said, pulling out a piece of rope. 'I knew there was something here somewhere! Ask Mr Cooper to help you bring the horse back, if he thinks it's safe.'

They walked the dogs back down to where the trail ended. The path through the bush was easier to see now they'd been back and forth a few times. 'I'll keep the dogs out of the way up here,' said Hannah's mum.

Ellie raced through the trees with her bag of carrot sticks and grass, and the rope. She was almost afraid that Silvie would have disappeared, but the horse was still there, with Hannah stroking her nose.

'I was patting her for you while you were gone!'

'I patted Peanut for you too,' said Ellie. And she knew her friend understood how much Ellie wanted to be with the horse for every minute that she could, while she could still pretend it was hers.

She took a carrot stick from the bag and held it out with her hand flat. Silvie's warm lips brushed against her palm, and the carrot stick disappeared. *I'm feeding a horse!* Ellie thought.

It was just as fun the second time, but she gave the next carrot stick to Hannah.

Hannah fed it to the horse and grinned. 'Horses are nearly as good as dogs,' she teased.

The grass was harder to feed because it kept blowing off their hands, but Hannah's dad said taking the horse up to the picnic ground was a good idea. He tied the rope to Silvie's halter and she looked up, waiting to be led.

'I think she'll be happy to get out of here,' he said. He pulled out his big silver pocketknife, unfolded the pliers, and cut the wire. Together, they rolled the fence back out of the way.

With Mr Cooper holding onto the end of the rope, Ellie led the horse back to the grassy picnic spot. Hannah and her mum followed, keeping the dogs well out of the way, even though Silvie didn't seem afraid of them now that she wasn't stuck in a fence. For the next hour, she grazed all around the clearing, with Ellie beside her.

Ellie had never been so happy.

CHAPTER 8

hen Mona saw where they'd found Silvie, she said it wasn't safe for her to stay there, and that she would have to take her back to Rainbow Street. She put up a notice on a tree, with the shelter's phone number in big clear printing.

The grey mare abandoned here has been taken into custody by the Rainbow Street Shelter. If you have any information about this horse, please contact us immediately.

'Why would someone leave her here?' Ellie asked.

'I can't figure it out,' Mona said. 'Maybe they just didn't have any place to keep her – but there's no point hiding her out here and not looking after her.'

'Maybe she was stolen!' said Hannah.

'It's too bad she's not that stolen racehorse,' said Hannah's dad. 'You might have got a reward, Ellie!'

Ellie smiled. She knew exactly what reward she'd have asked for: to go for a ride. A proper ride, not just sitting on the horse's back for three seconds before sliding down her neck.

Mona had hay in the horse float, and Silvie walked right in. But once she was in there, she kept looking around behind her, as if she was waiting for something.

'Are you used to having another horse with you?' Mona asked her. 'Never mind; you can share the yard with Bessy until we find a better place for you.'

'Will she like her?' Ellie asked anxiously. Bert had told her that the goat was always the boss when other goats or sheep came to stay.

'If they don't look happy when they meet, we'll separate them,' Mona reassured her. 'But horses like company, and so does Bessy.' She locked the tailgate of the float.

'Come on, girls!' called Hannah's mum as she loaded the dogs into the car. 'The adventure's over for the day!'

Ellie didn't want the adventure to end. She didn't want the horse to disappear out of her life. Hannah might be able to tell her what happened to Silvie, but Ellie needed to know for herself.

'Could I please visit her at your shelter?' she asked.

Mona smiled. 'I can't very well say no to the person who rescued her! As long as you remember that she won't be there forever. If she can't go back to her owner, we'll have to find her a new home.'

Ellie nodded.

Ellie nodded again that night, when her mum sat beside her on her bed and said, 'I know that Hannah's parents let her have a dog after she worked at Rainbow Street – but a horse really is different. We can't keep a horse in the backyard, and we can't afford to pay someone else to look after one.'

'Maybe we could think about getting a dog,' said her dad.

Ellie fell asleep thinking about the feeling of Peanut lying beside her in her bed at Hannah's house, and the fun of running along the trail with Molly on her leash. But it was horses that galloped through her dreams, just like they always did.

CHAPTER 9

llie woke up fizzing with excitement. First thing this morning, she was going to Rainbow Street to visit the horse. 'My horse,' she said to herself, but very quietly, because she knew that would never be true.

'The shelter won't even be open yet,' said her mum, as she picked up the newspaper. 'There's plenty of time for breakfast!'

Ellie's parents always read the paper with their breakfast on Sunday mornings. Sometimes they found so many interesting things to read and discuss that they forgot to eat.

Ellie sighed, and got out her *Horses of the World* book. She'd studied it so often she thought she knew every type of horse there was, but a real horse was different from a picture. She wanted to figure out everything she could about the mysterious horse from the ravine.

She was glad she'd given Silvie a girl's name, even before Mona had told her that she was a mare. Ellie flicked through the book as she ate her cereal. Silvie's face didn't look like an Arabian's, and she was too small to be a thoroughbred or a draft horse.

'The police have found that stolen horse!' her dad exclaimed.

For once, Ellie was happy to listen to him reading the paper aloud.

Master Midnight, the champion race-horse stolen from his stable on Thursday night, was recovered late on Saturday, when the thieves' truck broke down just as they were about to deliver him to a large racing stud.

Unfortunately the stallion's companion pony, Pebbles, has not yet been found. His owner, Mrs Barrington, reports that

> Midnight is extremely distressed and will not settle down without her. It is feared that he will be unable to race in the Melbourne Cup this year unless the companion pony is returned.

'Does it say what the pony looks like?' asked Ellie's mum. 'It could be the one you found, Ellie!'

Ellie shook her head. 'She's bigger than a pony. She's a horse.'

'The paper's more interested in how much the racehorse is worth,' said Ellie's dad. 'It doesn't say any more about the pony.'

'The poor pony!' exclaimed Ellie. She imagined the lost, lonely Shetland, far from home and miserable without her friend.

It took Ellie's parents so long to get ready to leave that Ellie thought Silvie might have gone to a new home before they even got to the shelter.

But the silver horse and the three-legged goat were grazing side by side in the front yard. Ellie let out a sigh of relief.

Mona came out the red door and shook hands

with Ellie's parents. 'Did your daughter tell you she saved that horse's life?'

'We're very proud of her,' said Ellie's dad.

But Ellie wanted to hear about Silvie.

'We haven't found out anything about the mare yet,' said Mona. 'The vet will give her a proper check-up tomorrow morning, but apart from the cut on her face, she seems healthy. She's a lovely, calm horse – doesn't seem to be upset by everything's that's happened to her.'

'So you're sure it's safe for Ellie to go and pat her?' asked Ellie's mum.

'And groom her?' Ellie asked.

'You've always got to be careful with any animal,' said Mona. 'But since Ellie handled her yesterday without any trouble, it should be okay.'

Mona got a rope lead, a carrot and a horse brush from the storeroom, and they all went out to see the white horse.

Silvie came right away, nickering gently when she saw the carrot. Mona let Ellie feed it to her, then slipped a soft halter over the mare's head and tied her to the fence with a rope.

'Horses like to be brushed with long, smooth

strokes,' Mona said, brushing down Silvie's neck from head to shoulder. 'See how I'm brushing in the same direction her hair grows?'

Ellie nodded, following Mona's brush strokes with her hand. The horse stood relaxed, her ears pricked slightly forward.

'She likes that,' Mona smiled, and handed Ellie the brush.

Ellie brushed the horse's shoulders and sides, gently at first, and then more firmly when she felt Silvie relaxing and nodding in rhythm with the long strokes of the brush. The smell of horse filled her nose again; she breathed it in deep so she could keep it forever. White hairs floated onto her red T-shirt, and a butterfly thought danced inside her head: *I'm brushing a horse!* And another thought, fluttering around it: *One day I'll have my own horse to brush.*

Mona went back inside. Ellie's parents got their deck chairs out of the car and set them up in the garden. Ellie didn't notice. She and the horse were in their own world, and as long as she went on brushing, nothing could hurt them.

Bert came in the gate, and Bessy rushed up to

him, butting him gently till the old man gave her a piece of lettuce from the bag he was carrying.

'Where did you come from?' he asked Silvie, walking across to pat her. Ellie told him the story.

'Do you know what happened to her tail?' he asked.

'It was like this when I found her,' said Ellie.

'I think we need to talk to Mona,' said Bert. He went inside.

Ellie went on brushing, but she had a feeling that she and Silvie weren't in their own little world any longer. She brushed even harder when Bert came back out, because she didn't think she wanted to hear what he had to say.

'You've heard about the stolen racehorse, Midnight?' he asked.

'And they stole a pony too,' said Ellie. 'Has someone found it?'

'I think you have,' said Bert.

CHAPTER 10

'But this is a horse!' said Ellie. 'She's big!'

Bert smiled. 'You're right. She's an Australian stock horse. But if her job is to keep a racehorse company, she's called a companion pony. I think that's exactly what she is.'

Ellie wondered how Bert could tell so much about the horse just by looking at her.

'I went to see Midnight race last year,' he said, as if he'd guessed her question. 'I didn't get a good look at the horse that led him out of the stables, but it was about this size, and white.'

Mona came out. 'I've phoned the police,' she said. 'They'll contact—' Her phone rang before she could finish.

Everyone was very quiet as she answered it. 'That's right,' she said, 'an Australian Stock Horse. Grey; probably just under fifteen hands high.' She hung up, grinning. 'Pebbles?' she said. Silvie's ears twitched. 'Your owner will be here in an hour.'

The last of the perfect Ellie-and-Silvie world crumpled and fell away.

Part of Ellie was really truly glad that the horse was going back to a good home with people who cared about her, and a horse friend who was missing her.

But part of her wished that she could have had a bit longer to go on pretending that the horse was Silvie, and was hers.

'Can I still brush her?' she asked.

'Of course!' said Mona.

Ellie started brushing again, long hard strokes along the horse's back to the solid curve of the rump. She wasn't ready to say goodbye yet, but she knew she was going to cry if she didn't do something.

The funny thing was, that the longer she brushed, the harder it was to feel sad.

Ellie's dad went out to buy her a smoothie.

'Come and sit down,' called her mum. 'You need a rest.'

'I got strawberry,' said her dad.

Ellie sat on her mother's lap and drank the smoothie. Strawberry was her favourite, but she hardly tasted it. She suddenly felt so tired she wanted to cry. Her arms ached, and it felt good when her mum rubbed her shoulders.

But the hour was nearly gone already, and soon the horse would go too. Ellie didn't want to waste any of that precious time. She watched Pebbles and tried to memorise her from velvety nose to chopped-off tail.

'Her mane's all tangled!' she said. Seeing it was like a pin popping her bubble of pride at knowing about horses. *Maybe I'll never learn to be a horse person!* she thought. *Maybe I'll never have a horse, even when I grow up.*

But I've still got Silvie a little longer! said another thought.

She raced back to the horse. No matter how hard she tried to brush out the silver mane, the brush skimmed over the coarse hairs. The bristles were simply too soft to untangle the snarls.

'It's not fair!' Ellie said. Hot tears spurted in her eyes, and she brushed them away angrily. 'I want her to look perfect when the owner comes!'

'Try this,' said Bert. He combed Pebbles' forelock and the top of her mane with a metal comb, and handed it to Ellie.

It worked. And Ellie was just combing out the last tangles when a four-wheel drive and horse float pulled up in front of the gate. She put her face against Pebbles' shoulder and breathed in deep.

'Goodbye, Silvie,' she whispered.

Suddenly she knew that she couldn't bear to see the horse be taken away. She didn't even want to see the owner. She raced into the little blue house and shut herself in the bathroom.

Ellie didn't know how long she'd been in there when someone knocked on the door, but it was long enough that she was hiccupping more than crying.

'Are you ready to come out?' her mother asked.

Ellie opened the door, and her mum hugged her hard. 'Mrs Barrington wants to meet you,' she said.

'I don't want to,' Ellie muttered.

Her mum ran some water into the sink. 'Wash your face and you'll feel better,' she said.

Ellie washed the tears away and dried her face. She still didn't want to see the owner take Pebbles away, but she knew she had to.

Bert and Mona were waiting outside with Ellie's dad and a small woman in jeans and riding boots. The woman shook Ellie's hand as if she was a grown-up.

'Thank you,' she said. Her eyes were full of tears. 'If you hadn't found Pebbles when you did ... It's just too horrible to think about!'

Ellie didn't want to imagine it either. 'I'm glad I found her,' she said at last. 'She's a nice horse.'

'One of the best,' Mrs Barrington agreed. 'Pebbles has been one of the family for years, long before she became Midnight's companion. She taught my kids to ride when they were little, and she's teaching my nieces and nephews now.'

Ellie thought of how the mare had let her climb on her back, even when she was trapped and terrified. She couldn't help feeling jealous of the nieces and nephews.

'So, thank you, thank you, thank you from my whole family!' Mrs Barrington said again. She waved goodbye, turned down the path and climbed into her car.

Ellie waved back, watching the back of Pebbles' head as the horse float disappeared down the road. Her parents folded up their chairs.

'Thank you from us too,' Mona said to Ellie. 'I know it's sometimes hard to see an animal leave – but you can see why it's also rewarding.'

Ellie and her parents went back to the car. But before they could get in, the four-wheel drive and float pulled in behind them. Mrs Barrington jumped out.

'Wait!' she shouted. 'I was so happy to see Pebbles, I completely forgot about the reward!'

CHAPTER 11

e're very proud of Ellie,' her dad said, 'but she doesn't need a reward for doing the right thing.'

'The reward was announced on the news this morning,' said Mrs Barrington. 'It wouldn't be honest if I didn't give it.'

'Hannah's family helped too, and Mona came to pick her up,' said Ellie.

'Okay,' said Pebbles' owner. 'We'll get everybody together and work it out. But you were particularly brave, and I still want to thank you. Is there anything you'd like?'

Ellie had been waiting for this wish all her life. 'Could I please have a ride on Pebbles?'

Mrs Barrington smiled. 'I'm sure Pebbles

would be very happy about that. Come to the stables tomorrow afternoon.'

The stables on the hill were white and cheerful in the sunlight. The paddocks around them were green, with white wooden fences. And every paddock had a horse, or two horses, or mares with foals, or a herd of yearlings.

If a genie had given Ellie three wishes to design the most perfect place in the world, this was exactly how she'd have created it.

Mrs Barrington gave Ellie a tour of the stables. Racehorses looked out over the half doors of their stalls, ears twitching as Mrs Barrington spoke to each one.

Midnight and Pebbles were in the last stall. Pebbles was already saddled and bridled, and Mrs Barrington's teenage daughter Amy was cinching up Midnight's saddle.

'Ready?' asked Mrs Barrington, and she led Pebbles out while Amy followed with Midnight.

Then, Amy on Midnight and Ellie on Pebbles, they rode down the track, while the adults sat and talked.

Riding was just as perfect as Ellie had dreamed it would be. It was as thrilling as riding a bicycle down a hill, and as free as running on a beach with a dog, but it was different and better than both of them. It was the best thing she'd ever done in her life.

And now that she'd done it once, she wanted to do it again and again.

When the ride was finally over, Ellie kissed Pebbles' nose goodbye. 'Thank you!' she whispered, and she was sure the horse understood.

'See you next week!' said Amy.

'Next week?' asked Ellie.

'Next week,' echoed her mum, coming up to meet her. 'That's one of the things we've been talking about.'

And so, every Sunday afternoon, except when Pebbles was away steadying Midnight for an important race, Ellie's mum or dad drove her up to the stables for a riding lesson.

Hannah came a few times, but Peanut wasn't allowed at the stables, so she decided she'd rather go to the beach with him. Her family gave their share of the reward to the Rainbow Street Shelter. 'Because if it wasn't for them, we'd never have known how good it was to have a dog,' said Hannah's mum.

But Ellie's reward was different.

At the end of Ellie's tenth lesson, Mrs Barrington said she had something to tell her. Her voice was solemn, and for a moment Ellie was afraid she was going to say that she couldn't come back anymore.

But Mrs Barrington's eyes were smiling. 'Now that I know you're serious about riding, and have a feel for horses,' she said, 'I've got something to show you.'

She took Ellie to a paddock where six colts were grazing. Five were tall and rangy, browns and bays, but the smallest and stockiest was a silvery grey. 'This is Pebbles' son,' said Mrs Barrington. 'He's only two years old now, but when he's properly trained in a couple of years, you'll be ready to ride him.'

Ellie was barely listening. She couldn't stop looking at the colt – he was even more beautiful than his mother.

'What's his name?' she asked.

'Silver Shadow,' said Mrs Barrington. 'But you can change it if you want.'

Ellie wondered if she'd heard right. It almost sounded as if ... But that was impossible. She was crazy even to think it.

Mrs Barrington put her hand on Ellie's shoulder. 'I know you don't have room in your backyard for a horse, but he can go on living here for as long as you want.'

Ellie couldn't move or speak. She could barely even breathe.

'He's yours,' said Mrs Barrington.

**Bella the
Bored Beagle**

CHAPTER 1

One night when everyone else was asleep, a floppy-eared, brown-and-white dog was wide awake, ruffling the rug in her nesting box. When she started having her puppies, her owner got up to sit beside the box, stroking the labouring beagle when she got tired and telling her what a good little mother she'd be.

Five hours later, six puppies were nestled in the box beside her. They were all black-and-white, except for their round pink noses. The mother dog had licked them clean till they squirmed, and snuggled around them so they could drink her milk. Now they were resting after the adventure of being born, making newborn-puppy squeaks as they squirmed against their sleeping mother.

The owner knew the mother dog wouldn't want anyone to touch them, so she just sat, watching quietly.

'Six perfect little beagles!' she said. 'I wish I could keep you all! But you'll make whoever buys you very happy.'

She hoped that selling them would make her some money too, but right now she just cared that they were all healthy and perfect.

The prettiest of all was the one who'd been born first. She was the first one to feed, and she was the strongest. As the puppies grew over the next weeks, she would always knock the others out of the way if she wanted to drink. The other puppies rolled and tumbled, and found another nipple.

'You're a bossy little girl!' the owner told her. 'Whoever chooses you will have to be very strong too.'

Kate and Justin had just got married and moved into an elegant apartment with a view of the ocean. They both worked long days in the city, and on the weekends they liked having breakfast at their favourite cafe by the pier.

One Saturday morning when they'd finished their coffee and French toast, they walked on down the boardwalk along the beach. It was chilly, but so bright and beautiful that lots of other people were out too, rollerblading or cycling, or walking their dogs.

'You know what would be perfect?' Kate said.

'A dog!' said Justin.

'We could go to the animal shelter in Rainbow Street,' said Kate. 'They must have lots of dogs there.'

'It'd be more fun to have a puppy that we can train the way we want,' said Justin.

They pulled out their phones and searched as they walked.

～～～～～～

CUTE BEAGLE PUPPIES!

～～～～～～

Four males and two females. All tricolour (black, brown and white).

Five weeks old: ready to leave their
mum in three weeks.

Come and see them now – be ready
to fall in love!

The picture showed the cutest puppies Kate or
Justin had ever seen.

'Gorgeous!' said Kate.

Justin was already calling. 'Can we see them
today?' he asked.

The puppies were even cuter in real life. The
black on their faces was fading to brown, and
their pink puppy noses were now black. Their fur
was soft as velvet.

They staggered around on their short bowed
legs, yipping with shrill puppy squeals as they
tried to chase a soft blue ball. Sometimes they
wobbled into each other and stopped to wrestle
instead.

'They're all adorable!' Kate exclaimed.

'But she's the cutest!' Justin said, pointing to
the bossy firstborn puppy.

They watched as she shouldered through the

pack to get the blue ball. She hit it with her nose, jumping back in surprise when it rolled away. One of her brothers bumped into her and they both tumbled over. The little girl puppy rolled back to her feet and started after the ball again.

'She's smart!' said Justin.

'And beautiful,' said Kate, as the owner picked the puppy up and put it into her waiting arms. 'You're the sweetest little girl ever, aren't you?'

Smiling at each other over the puppy's head, Justin and Kate stroked the floppy velvet ears and the round bulgy belly. The baby beagle chewed on their fingers, wriggled against them and licked their faces: even her sour-milk puppy breath smelled sweet.

It made the beagle breeder happy to see people falling in love with one of her puppies. She knew this dog was going to a good home.

'Her name is Bella,' said Kate.

'Because she's so beautiful,' Justin agreed. They had been studying Italian, and *bella*, for beautiful, was one of the first words they had learned.

'How are we going to wait three whole weeks before we take her home?' Kate asked. She could hardly bear to put the puppy down again, even though the mother dog was anxious and Bella was squirming.

'You can visit again next weekend,' said the owner.

CHAPTER 2

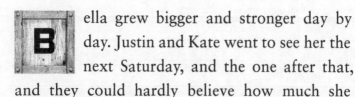ella grew bigger and stronger day by day. Justin and Kate went to see her the next Saturday, and the one after that, and they could hardly believe how much she changed each time.

The puppies could run and were starting to climb and jump up on things. And Bella was still the strongest, prettiest and smartest of all.

Tomorrow she was going to be eight weeks old, and Kate and Justin were going to take her home.

That night after work they went to a pet warehouse to buy Bella a soft comfy dog bed. It was pink with a pattern of white bones, and as

304

they walked around the pet store they filled it up with toys. They chose a soft baby ball for her to roll, a teddy bear to comfort her when she was alone, and a squeaky rubber bone for her to chew.

They bought a water dish, a food dish, a red collar and soft leash; special puppy food, puppy treats, and a sack of pee pads to put in the bathroom, for when they were at work and couldn't take Bella outside.

On Saturday morning they were too excited about getting their new puppy to go out for breakfast. They had toast and coffee, tidied the kitchen, and were ready to go.

Kate sighed with happiness. The sun was shining in the windows; the apartment was clean and polished. Soon their beautiful puppy would be in her little pink bed in the corner, and their lives would be even more perfect than they were now.

Another car was already at the beagle breeder's when Kate and Justin arrived.

'We were lucky we chose Bella first!' Kate whispered as they walked to the door.

Luckily, the other family seemed very happy too. They had a boy and a girl, and they'd chosen a boy and a girl puppy. 'The pups will be company for each other during the day,' they told Kate and Justin, 'and the kids will give them lots of exercise.'

'Beagles do need lots of exercise!' the owner agreed. 'And you'll need to be firm with them and start some puppy training right away.'

She kissed each puppy on the top of its smooth little head as she handed it to its new owners. 'They've already had their first lot of shots,' she explained. 'You'll have to take them to your own vets for the next ones in a couple of weeks. But love's the most important thing – lots of play and lots of love should give you long and happy lives together.'

Kate and Justin were ready to give the puppy just as much love as she needed.

Bella sat on Kate's lap on the way home. For the first ten minutes she snuggled and squirmed, trying to climb up to lick Kate's face. Then she tried to waddle across to Justin. For the last five minutes she squirmed as if she couldn't get comfortable. Finally, as they pulled into their parking space, she threw up.

'I should have brought a towel,' said Kate, wiping vomit off her new jeans with a tissue.

Justin took the puppy, snapped the little collar in place, and clipped on the leash. 'We'd better keep her outside till she's finished.' He put her down on the grass.

Bella had never worn a collar before, but she didn't seem to mind. She didn't even seem to mind that she'd just been sick. She waddled around the grass, sniffing and squeaking.

'I wonder if she has to pee?' Justin asked.

'Let's wait a bit longer,' said Kate.

Bella was too busy to pee – there were new smells to sniff and new things to see. She yipped at a boy on a skateboard, cowered at the hiss of a bus opening its doors, and bounded over to people walking past. Nearly everyone stopped to smile and say, 'She's so cute!'

Justin and Kate felt very proud as they carried their new puppy up to their home.

An hour later, Bella had peed on the floor, tipped

over her water dish, chewed the ends off the laces of Justin's sneakers, and finally fallen asleep in the middle of the floor.

Kate picked her up and laid her gently in the pink-and-white-bone bed.

'She looks so sweet when she's asleep,' said Kate.

'The breeder said she'd need about twenty hours of sleep a day – she'll probably sleep for ages,' said Justin.

They tucked the teddy bear in beside the peaceful puppy, closed the door quietly and went out for lunch.

Bella slept for nearly an hour. Then a door slammed in the apartment upstairs. She woke up and found herself alone.

Bella had never been alone before. She'd never been away from her mother and brothers and sisters. She started to cry. She whined and yipped, and then she howled.

Howling felt good for a while, but when she

was bored with it she chewed gently on her teddy bear. The teddy bear fell over, so she growled and wrestled it out of the basket. It was bigger than her, but she dragged it around the floor until its ear came off.

She began to explore the apartment. Kate's furry slippers were beside the bed. They smelled of wool and Kate, and Bella began to chew.

CHAPTER 3

Every night after school, Timothy took Sherlock for a walk. Sometimes when his dad got home they all went for a long walk together, down to the beach or the leash-free park. But unless he had soccer practice, Tim always walked Sherlock first.

When his mother had moved out two years ago, Tim had hated coming home from school. Mrs Gunther, their neighbour, would meet him at the school gate and take him next door till his dad, Matt, got home from work.

Tim had lived next door to the Gunthers for as long as he could remember. They were like extra grandparents. But going home to Mrs

Gunther wasn't the same as going home to his mum. And when his dad got home it still wasn't the same, because Matt was as miserable as Tim, and the house felt sad and empty too, even when they were both there. But Sherlock had changed everything.

Sherlock was a beagle, and until three months ago he'd been a sniffer dog. He'd worked with Tim's dad at the airport, checking that people weren't bringing in any food or plants or animals that they weren't supposed to. It was a very important job, because if bugs or diseases came in with the food or plants, they could spread around the country. Sherlock had been good at it. He'd walk along beside Tim's dad, and if he smelled any plants or animals, he would sit down in front of the person and their bag.

'Show me,' Matt would say, and Sherlock would sniff at the pocket on the backpack, or the corner of the suitcase where the smell was coming from.

He could smell so well that sometimes he sat down in front of a bag that someone had used as a picnic bag the week before, even though there was no food in it now. He'd smelled dog treats that people had forgotten they had in their pocket, and chocolate bars they'd forgotten were in their bags.

But he'd also found lots of things that people knew they weren't allowed to bring in with them. He'd discovered papayas, grapes, lemons, mangoes, and nearly every other kind of fruit there was. Sometimes the fruit he found did have fruit flies or other bugs. He'd sniffed out sausages and salamis hidden in socks, seeds tucked into shoes, wooden carvings full of woodworm, and a giant python coiled in a suitcase.

On his eighth birthday, Sherlock had retired and come home to live with Tim and his dad. He was still a very good detective, but it was time for him to relax and enjoy being a dog, instead of working all day.

Tim's dad had been worried that Sherlock might be bored, but the beagle loved his new life just as much as he'd loved working. He slept in his basket in the living room, but every morning at six-thirty he woke Matt, and then Tim.

Now, when Tim came home, the house wasn't empty, because Sherlock was there waiting for him. He sniffed Tim up and down, as if he was finding out what the boy had been doing, who he'd seen and what he'd eaten. He did the same to Mrs Gunther when she came over to make a snack. No matter what Tim was eating, Sherlock was sure he needed some too. His eyes were so soft and pleading that it was very hard to say no.

'You know what your dad says,' Mrs Gunther reminded Tim when he tried to sneak Sherlock half a biscuit or a bit of cheese. 'Beagles love to eat, and it's very easy for them to get fat. It's not healthy for them!'

But sometimes she gave in to the begging eyes too, and cut a slice of apple or carrot for Sherlock. 'At least that's healthy,' she said when Tim saw her doing it.

The only bad part about Sherlock being retired was that Tim's dad didn't have a dog to work with anymore. All dogs sniff, but not every dog can learn to be a sniffer dog and work in a busy airport. They have to have lots of energy to work all day, be very smart about what they're sniffing for, and stay calm and friendly around the people they meet.

Right now, there wasn't another dog who could do all those things. So, until the right beagle was accepted for training, Matt had to do more paperwork and other jobs he didn't like as much.

Tim knew his dad wouldn't be happy again till he had a dog to work with.

By the time Bella was a year old, she had chewed up two left sneakers, one pair of sandals, one high-heeled boot, one pair of jeans, and more socks and underwear than Justin or Kate could count. She'd eaten sunglasses, remote controls, and the spines off a whole shelf of books.

She'd been to the Emergency Room when she couldn't stop vomiting after eating the lilies in a vase on the coffee table. She'd had another trip after she found a bowl of Easter eggs.

She had a chain leash now, because she liked to chew on it whenever she had to stop on a walk. She could eat through a soft leash while they waited for a green light to cross the road.

Justin and Kate didn't know that she'd even eaten the back seatbelts in the car.

One day they came home after leaving their bedroom door open and found the bedspread in the middle of the living room, white fluff scattered all over the apartment, and an empty torn-up pillowcase in the bathroom. When they went to make the bed again, they noticed more white stuffing in the bedroom and a beagle-sized hole in the mattress.

After that they put Bella in a dog-crate when they were at work, but the neighbours complained that she howled most of the time she was in it.

Kate and Justin took turns jogging around the block with Bella before work, and again afterwards. They found a fenced dog park where they could let her run free, but Bella ran away as soon as she was let loose. Then they learned to throw a ball for her the instant they unclipped her leash. She'd always come back for her ball.

Bella loved playing ball. She liked jumping and catching it – but what she liked best was chasing and finding the ball after a long, hard throw. And even though she'd eaten lots of balls when she was home alone, she never lost one when she was playing. It didn't matter how deep into the bushes the ball went, Bella could always find it.

Sometimes, if the ball had landed in a mud puddle, or under a prickly bush, they threw her a new ball. Bella would rush to it, sniff it, and leave it there while she went on searching for the ball she wanted. They could never trick her.

They were so sure that she'd never run away if she had a ball to play with that they decided they could start taking her to a leash-free beach.

'Let's go on an adventure, Bella!' said Kate. And they drove to a beach with bushland between the highway and the sea. Kate sang and Bella wagged all the way.

But just as Kate picked up the ball-thrower and unclipped Bella's leash, a rabbit ran out of the bush. Bella bayed a deep hunting call and took off after it. Her nose was low to the ground, her tail was waving, and she was running so fast that in a moment she was out of sight.

Kate raced desperately after her. 'Bella,' she shrieked. 'BELLA!'

No beagle appeared.

She phoned Justin. He left work right away and came to help her hunt for their runaway dog. They ran up and down the beach and through the bush. Justin's voice was louder than Kate's, but it didn't make any difference – Bella didn't come back. Once Kate thought she heard her baying again, but they didn't ever see so much as the white tip of a beagle tail.

Finally, when it was dark and they couldn't run anymore, they went home.

Tim and his dad were at the airport. Usually Tim loved going to the airport. He felt proud when pilots said hi to his dad and smiled at him. And he liked saying hello to the other sniffer dogs. If they were wearing their jackets, they were working and he wasn't supposed to pat them, but it was okay if they weren't dressed yet.

Today Tim didn't feel like smiling or talking to anyone.

Today he was going to visit his mum all by

himself. His dad was going to put him on the plane, and his mum and her new husband and new baby would meet him when he landed.

A little part of him was excited about going on the plane, but another part was nervous. Even though his mum had moved so far away, and he only saw her in school holidays, he'd always thought that she'd come back to him and his dad one day. When she'd married her new husband he had to admit that wasn't true, and now that he had a baby brother, it hurt all over again.

Kate and Justin hardly slept all night. They got back to the beach just as the sun came up.

They ran through the bush by the beach where Bella had disappeared, calling and searching on different paths. Kate saw something brown behind a sand dune.

'BELLA!' she screamed. The brown lump didn't move. Kate's heart tightened. 'She's hurt! Please don't be dead, Bella!'

Justin raced back to her. Gasping for breath,

they ran around the dune, only to find someone's forgotten brown T-shirt crumpled at the bottom of a bush.

Kate burst into tears. Justin nearly did too. They didn't know if their beautiful dog was alive or dead, or whether she was somewhere near them or far away.

'We'll phone the pound and the vet,' said Justin. 'Someone might have found her already.'

CHAPTER 4

Bella had only seen the rabbit for an instant, but the moment she turned towards it, she hit its trail. She had never smelled anything like this. The scent of it poured into her wet black nose and flooded her body, a thousand times better than the smell of tennis balls or chewy treats. She couldn't see or hear anything else – the scent said, *Follow me!* and she obeyed.

Sometimes the trail circled, and sometimes it zigzagged through the scrub. When she came to a place where a second rabbit had run across the first rabbit's path, she followed the second one, because her nose told her this trail was fresher.

If she'd been a human, Bella would have said that she was happier than she'd ever been in her life. But she was a dog, so she didn't stop to think about being happy or about what she wanted to do. She just did it.

She ran and ran until she couldn't run any more. Her legs folded up and she collapsed on the ground. She was panting hard, her long tongue was lolling out of her mouth, and her heart was racing. She still hadn't caught a rabbit; she was hungry and very thirsty, but she was too exhausted to move.

The world was dark, and quiet. The little beagle stayed where she was, and went to sleep.

In the middle of the night, the full moon came out from behind a cloud. It beamed white onto the sand, lit up the hollows and spaces in the scrub, and shone into Bella's eyes.

She stretched and stood up. For a minute she felt lonely and lost, but after that she was too thirsty to worry about anything else.

Water glinted below her. Bella trotted through the bush, across the sand to the sea and lapped up a great mouthful of salt water.

It tasted terrible. She shook her head in disgust and tried again. It tasted even worse.

Bella gave up and trotted on down the beach. The salt water in her belly made her vomit, but then she found a dead fish at the tideline. It stank, but Bella liked stinky smells, so when she'd eaten it, she rolled in the seaweed it had been lying in.

Back up near the bush, she found half an ice-cream cone, still soggy with melted ice-cream. Bella ate that quickly – and a moment later she smelled rabbit.

She forgot that she was thirsty and tired. Her nose was telling her to run, and she ran. The rabbit led her in long looping circles through the darkness, and when it finally disappeared down a hole, Bella was further than ever from where Kate had last seen her.

She collapsed under another bush and slept till dawn, her body twitching with exhaustion.

The next time Bella woke up, she trotted the other way through the bush, towards the highway. She licked up pools of dew on the footpath and found some soggy chips in a crumpled bag. She was ready to go home.

The morning rush of traffic had begun. Cars and trucks were hurtling along the highway towards the city. Bella stood on the curb; finally she gave up waiting and rushed onto the road.

A car swerved and honked. Bella raced back to the side, her tail tucked tight with fear, and ran back into the scrub above the beach. A little later she bayed joyfully, and started on the scent of a new rabbit.

Kate phoned the City Pound while Justin called their local vet. 'Beagles can run a long way,' they were both warned. 'But we'll call you as soon as we hear anything.'

They hugged each other tight, and went to work. They knew it was going to be a long and miserable day.

An hour later, a jogger with a bull terrier heard a dog barking in the bush. It wasn't a frightened bark, or saying, *Come play with me!* Even though the man had never known a beagle, he was sure it was a hunting bark.

His own dog was old, and obedient. He'd unclipped her leash because she could be trusted to trot along beside him and not run away. But her ears pricked now and she veered off the path towards the sound.

The man called her back, but when the other dog bayed again, closer, and he saw the white tip of a waving tail, he changed his mind. 'Okay,' he told his dog, 'let's see what's happening.'

A second later, Bella raced across the path in front of them. She was filthy, stinky and skinny after her day and night of running. She was very obviously lost.

'Come here, girl,' the man called.

Bella kept on running.

He called again. She didn't seem to hear.

'SIT!' the man shouted, and Bella was so surprised that she sat. So did his dog.

'Stay,' the man ordered, more quietly. 'Good dog.'

Offering her a dog biscuit from his pocket, he clipped his dog's lead onto Bella's collar.

With the panting beagle on the leash, and his own bull terrier trotting obediently behind, they walked back to his car. He loaded the two dogs in and drove to the Rainbow Street Shelter.

CHAPTER 5

he man left his own dog in the car and led Bella into the waiting room.

'Can I help you?' asked a cockatoo on a perch above the desk.

'Wow!' said Mona. 'That is one filthy beagle!'

'I found her running in the bush by the beach,' the man explained. 'I think she was hunting.'

'She smells like she caught a dead fish,' said Mona, crinkling her nose. 'You're going to need a bath, little girl! But first let's check if you've been microchipped!'

The man waited while Mona ran a wand over Bella's shoulder. It beeped, and Mona cheered.

'What happens now?' the man asked.

'I'll call the pet registry. They'll be able to look up who the owner is, and tell them their dog is here.'

'So she'll be okay?'

'I'm sure it'll all work out,' said Mona. 'She's a beautiful little dog under all that muck. I imagine her owner will be overjoyed to have her back.'

But when Justin and Kate turned up at Rainbow Street that afternoon, they weren't so sure that they did want their beautiful little beagle back.

'We've been so worried!' said Kate, as Bella bounced around them. 'But she's not even sorry!'

'Dogs don't feel sorry for something that happened yesterday,' Mona explained. 'She's just happy to see you now.'

In fact, Bella was very excited because she'd smelled the guinea pigs in the SMALL ANIMAL ROOM and the rabbits in their enclosure. The shelter was a paradise of smells, and she was sniffing all of them.

'We never knew a dog would be this much trouble,' said Justin. 'We've tried to look after her, but she goes on destroying things and running away.'

'The problem is that beagles get bored easily,' Mona said. 'They find it very hard to be left alone inside all day.'

'I wish we'd known that when we bought her!' said Kate. 'But I can't bear to think of giving her away.'

'We might have to move if we don't,' said Justin. 'The neighbours are sick of her howling and barking.'

Mona was listening carefully. She felt sorry for them, but her job here was to think about the animals first.

'Bella needs a home where she's busy all day, with other dogs or people around. She needs lots of exercise and play, and some discipline – she has to know that she's not the boss and that she can't destroy your things.'

'I don't think we can give her that,' Kate said softly. Justin shook his head in agreement.

'If you decide to leave her with us,' Mona said,

'I'll make very sure that the new owners understand what she needs before I let them take her.'

Kate and Justin looked at each other, their eyes filling with tears. They hugged their dog, and went home without her.

Bella's tail drooped as she watched them go. Mona sighed. She was sure it was the right thing to do, but that didn't stop her from feeling sad.

She led Bella out to the dog yard, picking up a tennis ball on the way. The beagle started dancing around her, leaping for the ball.

'Down!' Mona said sternly, but she was smiling as she shut the gate.

Bella didn't seem to notice the other dogs in their kennels. All she could focus on was the ball.

'You're going to be okay,' Mona told her, making her sit and wait till she threw the ball. 'You just need something to do.'

CHAPTER 6

Tim was hoping his mum would be on her own when she met him at the airport. For just that little while, he wanted to pretend she was his mum and nobody else's, just the way she used to be.

They were all there though, waiting at the gate for him. He saw his mum hand the baby to her new husband, and then she was rushing towards him with her arms open wide, and hugging him tight, tight, tight.

'Look how tall you are!' she exclaimed when she finally let him go. 'You've grown so much!'

She took his hand, and led him across to her husband and baby. 'Do you want to hold your brother?'

NO! Tim shouted inside.

He didn't say it. The baby was very little. His name was Bentley, but he seemed too little to have a grown-up name – he was only ten days old. Tim didn't think he'd ever seen such a brand-new baby. He was afraid he'd drop him, and his mum would be angry – but he knew it would hurt her feelings if he didn't try.

The baby was wrapped up like a parcel in a soft blue blanket, with only his silvery-fuzzed head sticking out. Gently and carefully, Tim's stepdad put the bundle into Tim's arms. His mum hovered at his side. 'Hold him like this,' she said, placing Tim's hand behind the baby's head.

Tim looked down into his sleeping brother's round pink face. He smelled of baby powder and milk; his wet lips opened and shut, blowing bubbles like a goldfish. It was hard to believe that he was going to be a real person one day.

But it was hard to be angry with him too; hard to be jealous of something so small and helpless. Holding him made Tim feel a bit the way he did when Sherlock looked at him with his big brown eyes.

He was very relieved when his mum lifted the bundle out of his arms again, and tucked the baby against her own shoulder.

Bella would have been happy for Kate and Justin to come and take her home, but she was happy at Rainbow Street too. From her run she could see and hear ten other dogs in their own runs, and the birds in an aviary. Her nose twitched with all the different scents of the other animals, whether she could see them or not: dogs, goats, cats, rabbits and birds. And she could watch Bert and Mona as they went in and out the back door.

Of course, she liked it best when they came into the dog yard, and best of all when they came to spend time with her.

The first job was to have her checked by a veterinarian to make sure she was healthy.

'Very healthy!' said the vet.

Next Bert and Mona needed to play with her and find out if she knew how to come, sit and stay.

Bella did know how, but she only did those things when she felt like it, because Kate and Justin had felt so guilty about her being left alone during the day that they just played with her when they got home. They'd thought she would be bored if she had to practise sitting, staying or coming when she was called.

But Bella loved treats. She loved any food.

And so when Bert took her out to the dog lawn, Bella loved the games of getting a tiny treat every time she sat, or when Bert let her go at one side of the lawn and Mona called her at the other. Sometimes she got a bit of dog biscuit for that, and sometimes she got to play with the ball.

She learned very, very fast.

'You're a smart little girl,' Mona told her. 'You just don't have enough to do.'

'She'll need a family that can keep her really busy,' said Bert.

'People with kids,' Mona suggested.

So the next job was to find out for sure if she was gentle with people and other dogs. They watched how she behaved when people came to the shelter to look at the dogs who were ready to be adopted and see if there was one who'd be right for them.

Bella always came to the front of her run, wagging her tail. Even a little boy who banged on her gate with his toy truck didn't frighten her.

Even though she had her own dog now, Hannah still came to Rainbow Street after school on Tuesdays to help clean out the runs and cages, feed the animals and pat them – and play with the dogs. That was her favourite part.

'This one loves playing ball,' said Bert. 'I reckon you could train her to do anything for a ball game!'

Hannah threw the ball as hard as she could, up and down the yard. Bella caught it every time. Back and forth she ran, dropping the ball at Hannah's feet and leaping with impatience for the girl to throw it again.

Bert was sitting outside one of the other dog runs with a fluffy little black dog with a grey muzzle. She was too old to care about ball games, and Bert rubbed her head soothingly as he watched Hannah and Bella.

'Now you've got some of that beagle bounce out of her,' he said to Hannah, 'do you want to try some training?'

With the fluffy dog following faithfully at his heels, he scooped up a handful of dry dog food for treats. 'Come on, Miss Muppet,' he said, 'you show Bella how to sit.'

The old dog sat obediently for her treat.

'Your turn,' Bert said to Hannah.

'Sit, Bella!' Hannah said. She'd trained Peanut to sit, stay and come when he was still a puppy, but she knew it would take longer for Bella, since she was already grown-up.

Bella sat, her eyes fixed on Bert's hand. Bert gave Hannah her own supply of treats, and she gave one to Bella. 'Good dog!'

'We've been working on that one,' Bert said proudly.

They practised that twice more. Bella's eyes were shining. She loved getting treats, but she loved being told she was a good dog even more.

'Too easy!' said Bert. 'Watch this, Bella!' He told the old dog to stay, walked halfway across the yard, and returned. Miss Muppet watched him all the way, but stayed sitting till he got back and gave her a treat and a cuddle.

'Sit, Bella!' Hannah said again. 'Now, stay!' She took two steps away from the dog, then stepped back and gave her the treat. Bella waggled all over with joy at being patted and praised.

Hannah tried taking three steps, but this time Bella was so excited that she leapt after the girl. 'No,' said Hannah, and started again. After six more tries, Bella could sit and stay while Hannah walked ten steps away.

'I think she's earned another game!' said Bert. 'We want to stop the training before she's bored, so she always thinks it's fun.' He handed the ball back to Hannah.

Hannah tossed the ball from hand to hand, thinking about how to make the game more challenging.

Bella watched, her eyes bright.

'Sometimes I play hide-and-seek with Peanut,' said Hannah. 'Mum makes him stay with her till I call him – but there's not anywhere to hide here.'

'Great idea!' said Bert. He disappeared to the storeroom, with Miss Muppet trotting at his heels, and came back with a stack of cardboard boxes waiting to be recycled. 'How about a game of hide-the-ball?'

He scattered the boxes around the yard and then made Bella sit while Hannah hid the ball. Hannah raced back. 'Find the ball!'

Bella raced straight to the box, nosed it over, and bounded back to Hannah with the ball in her mouth. 'Clever girl!' said Hannah. 'Now fetch!' She threw the ball across the yard as hard as she could.

'Good thinking!' said Bert. 'She'd much rather have a ball game than a food reward.'

Bella wagged her tail *yes*, begging for another turn. This was her new favourite game. She trembled with excitement each time Bert made her sit while Hannah hid the ball, then shot across the yard to the boxes. Often she got the ball the first time, but if Hannah had hidden it under a pile, she just nosed each box off until she got to the right one.

'This is one smart little dog,' said Bert, and Bella wagged her tail as if she'd understood that too.

'Can I talk about Bella at the assembly on Monday?' Hannah asked Mona, when the game was over and Bella was back in her run. 'She's so adorable!'

'I thought you were going to choose another animal than a dog this time,' Mona said.

'I guess Bella's so pretty someone's going to want her soon,' Hannah admitted.

'And she needs a home that can manage her,' said Mona. 'I don't want someone to adopt her again just because she's cute.'

Hannah walked slowly through the SMALL ANIMAL ROOM, and the rabbit and cat enclosures. A lop-eared bunny watched her as she went past. 'Hi there, Willow!' she said, sitting down at the end of his run. The rabbit was shy with strangers, but he'd been at the shelter for a month now and had decided Hannah was a friend. He hopped slowly over till his head was nearly against her leg.

'Do you want a head massage?' Hannah asked,

stroking his long floppy ears and head. Willow had let her pat him before, but it was the first time he'd come right to her. Hannah moved very quietly and carefully; the rabbit's dark-blue eyes had closed, and she didn't want anything to disturb him now.

But when Mona came to the door, Willow woke up from his trance. He hopped around Hannah until she stood up too.

'He wants you to dance with him,' Mona called.

So Willow hopped around Hannah, twisting and kicking his heels in the air, and Hannah did her best to copy him. She laughed till her stomach ached.

'Okay, Willow!' she said when she could catch her breath again. 'It looks like I'm going to talk about you at the Monday assembly!'

CHAPTER 7

Tim missed Sherlock the whole week he was at his mum's. He missed his dad too, but it was almost too hard to think about his dad while he was with his mum and stepdad. They talked on the phone nearly every night, and Tim could tell his dad was working hard to sound happy, but he wasn't a good actor. 'I picked up a pizza on the way home,' Matt said on Friday night, 'with triple anchovies! Mmm, yum!'

'Ick, yuck!' said Tim, like he always did when his dad wanted anchovies on pizza.

And they both knew that they didn't care about the anchovies nearly as much as they did about eating the pizza together, because that was what they did on Friday nights. Sherlock usually had a taste too, when they each thought the other one wasn't looking.

Missing Sherlock was different. It was a simple kind of missing. Tim just wished he could put his arms around the dog's warm, solid body.

His mother didn't like dogs. She was always cleaning everything in case the baby got sick, and she said dogs weren't hygienic.

Tim thought she was right. Sherlock did all the unhygienic dog things she complained about: he licked his own bottom, sniffed telephone poles where other dogs had peed, and ate disgusting bits of squashed food on the footpath.

His mum never mentioned that dogs made the most revolting smells in the world, so Tim didn't tell her that Sherlock was a champion at them. He and his dad just groaned, 'Gross, Sherlock!' and opened the windows when that happened.

In fact, his mum didn't ask at all about Sherlock. They talked about school, and soccer, and his friends. And Bentley.

'Bentley's so lucky to have a big brother like

you!' she said. She showed Tim pictures of when he was a baby. 'See how much you two look alike! You'll be great friends when he's older.'

Tim couldn't really tell if he'd looked like his brother when he was a baby. They both had round pink faces sticking out of a blue-wrapped bundle. And right now, Bentley was just a baby who threw up every time he was fed and needed his nappies changed. He wasn't any more hygienic than Sherlock – and he was a lot less fun.

On Saturday afternoon, his stepdad looked after Bentley, and Tim and his mum went to the City Aquarium. They went on a glass-bottomed boat, and were given fish-feed pellets to throw in. Looking through the glass beneath their feet made it feel as if they were floating in the water with the hungry, brightly coloured fish, instead of riding on top.

At the next tank, the guide chose Tim to ring a bell. Four giant stingrays swam to the surface to be fed. Tim and his mum learned how to hold the fish, sticking out through their fists, so that the stingrays could take them before flapping away on their great white wings. One of them spurted water back at them: Tim laughed, and his mum didn't even complain that it wasn't hygienic.

When they'd seen nearly everything there was to be seen at the aquarium, they went out to lunch. Tim chose tacos, and they sat at a table all by themselves and his mum didn't say anything when the chilli sauce dripped onto his clean jeans.

On Sunday morning, it was just as hard saying goodbye to his mum as it had been saying goodbye to his dad the week before. Tim even felt a little bit sad about saying goodbye to Bentley.

Sherlock came with Matt to meet Tim at the airport. He must have felt confused, because he had to stay in the car instead of coming in to work. So, when Tim got to the car Sherlock sniffed him all over, and then sniffed his backpack all over, as if to prove he could still do it.

But he licked Tim's face too, and sniffer dogs never do that when they're working. He was very, very happy to have his boy home.

'Almost as happy as me!' Tim's dad laughed, and hugged him hard.

Tim hadn't seen his dad smiling this much for a long time. 'Are you getting another dog to work with?' he asked.

'Still waiting!' said his dad. 'There just aren't enough trained dogs to go around right now.'

'It's too bad Sherlock can't go to work with you sometimes.'

Matt rubbed the beagle's floppy ears. 'This boy's earned his retirement. And it's good having him at home, isn't it?'

Tim nodded. He would have hated it if Sherlock wasn't there when he got home from school every afternoon, or if the dog didn't wake him up with his wet beagle nose every morning. At his mum's house he woke up because Bentley was crying, and if the baby wasn't crying his mum tried to sleep in, so Tim had to stay in his room and be quiet. But Sherlock's funny face and wagging tail always made him laugh – and there was no point staying in bed, because he knew Sherlock would have already woken up his dad, and it was time to go for a walk.

In her run in the animal shelter, Bella was watching Bert. He was feeding all the dogs in turn, and there were still three more ahead of her. She was already drooling by the time he opened her gate.

'You're not hungry, are you, Bella?' Bert teased, hiding the scoop behind his back.

Bella licked her lips, nosing around his legs.

'Can't fool you!' he laughed. 'You'd sniff out food anywhere!'

CHAPTER 8

At the next Monday morning assembly, Hannah talked about Willow, the lop-eared rabbit. 'If you're thinking about a pet, you should go to the Rainbow Street Shelter and see him. He looks cute in this picture – but if you feel how soft he is, and see him doing his happy dance, you'll love him.'

Maybe Dad could have a sniffer rabbit, Tim thought, smiling at the thought of a bunny in a jacket checking the suitcases at the airport. Except it would probably only sniff out carrots.

He didn't tell Hannah his joke. She was walking into the classroom with her best friend, Ellie, and they never thought his jokes were funny.

But on Friday afternoon, when he looked

out the window and saw Mona from Rainbow Street walking through the playground with her dog Nelly, Tim suddenly remembered his sniffer-bunny joke again.

'I can't believe I never thought of it before!'

On Friday afternoons Mona brought Nelly to hear the little kids read. They all loved reading to the gentle brown-and-white dog, and even kids who weren't good readers, or who got nervous reading out loud to the teacher and other grown-ups, were happy to read to Nelly.

Tim could read easily now, but he knew why the little kids liked reading to Nelly. It was like telling Sherlock something – the dog never thought he was stupid, even when he'd done or said something that everyone else in the world would have said was dumb.

Maybe this idea was dumb too, but it was worth a try.

He was the first out of the classroom when the bell rang. He raced around to the door where the little kids came out. Mona was standing just inside, so the kids were all stopping to pat Nelly goodbye as they passed. Tim waited impatiently.

Finally, all the kids had straggled out. Mona and Nelly were walking out the door. Tim's mouth was dry.

Mona smiled at him. It was a nice smile. It made him feel safe, like he could ask her the craziest question and she wouldn't laugh.

'Do you ever get any beagles at the shelter?' he asked.

At nine o'clock on Saturday morning, Tim, his dad and Sherlock walked up the path to the cheery, cherry-red door under the bright, painted rainbow. They laughed at the cockatoo who thought he was the receptionist, said hello to Nelly, and then followed Mona through to the dog yard.

Sherlock trotted calmly beside Matt. There were eight other dogs, all barking hello, but the beautiful young beagle was the only one they noticed. They went straight to her run.

Bella play-bowed to Sherlock, with her nose on her front paws, her bottom in the air and her tail waving wildly.

'She's asking him to play,' Mona said, 'and telling him that she knows he's the boss.'

'Here, Bella!' said Tim's dad.

The beagle looked up and crossed to his side.

Sherlock wagged his tail. Matt smiled. Tim felt happiness bursting out all over his body.

'What happens if she can't be trained to be a sniffer dog?' asked Mona. 'I don't want the poor girl to come back here again.'

'We'll be happy to have two dogs at home, won't we, Tim?' said his dad. 'She'll be easier to control with an older dog at home with her during the day. And our yard's already beagle-proof. So whatever happens, Tim's idea is the best thing that's happened to me for a long time.'

So Matt adopted Bella, and two weeks later she went on her training course to become a sniffer dog.

If Tim hadn't known how badly his dad wanted a working dog again, he'd have hoped that Bella would fail her training so she could live with them. But he did know, so he was hoping nearly as much as his dad for her to pass.

Matt took Tim and Sherlock over to Rainbow Street one night after work, to tell Mona how Bella was going.

'She's excellent! She's a star!' he said. Tim rubbed Sherlock's ears, because he didn't want the old dog to get jealous.

'Well, her first owners will be very pleased to hear that,' said Mona. 'I can tell them tomorrow when they come to pick up their new friend.'

Even though Justin and Kate knew that they couldn't handle a lively dog like Bella, their apartment seemed empty with her gone. So they'd had a long talk with Mona about what pet would be right for them, and now they were building a rabbit hutch for Willow.

'Maybe you could let me know how the rest of Bella's training goes,' Mona added.

'I'd like that,' said Matt.

Training was the best fun Bella had ever had in her whole life. The only thing that Bella didn't like was being bored, and now she was busy, busy, busy all the time. Some of the dogs got distracted during the games, some got a bit stressed; some dogs didn't like being around so many people. All those dogs were sent home, but Bella and her clever beagle nose passed every test.

Now she'd live with the other sniffer beagles at night, and work with Tim's dad during the day. To celebrate her graduation, Tim and his dad, Sherlock, Nelly and Mona met for lunch and a walk on the beach.

On Bella's first day of work at the airport, she wore a jacket with an L for Learner. Tim's dad gave her an extra pat. 'Are you ready?' he asked, and Bella looked up at him, wagging her tail as they walked into the busy arrivals hall. She walked along the line of people collecting their suitcases, sniffing as she walked. She didn't need to stop to know that there were no food or plants in the bags. 'Nothing interesting,' her nose told her each time. Or: 'Sweaty clothes, tennis ball … but no food.'

Suddenly she smelled something interesting. There was food in a bag off to the side. Wagging her tail happily, Bella walked straight over to the woman holding the bag and sat down in front of her. People stared. The woman blushed.

'Would you mind opening your bag?' Matt said, putting on his rubber gloves. Then he pulled an apple core out of the side pocket.

'Good girl!' he said to Bella, giving her a chewy treat. 'Clever dog!'

Bella gobbled it.

The woman said, 'I was eating the apple when I got off the plane, and I couldn't see a bin, so I just dropped the core into my bag. I didn't think it would matter.'

'It matters,' said Tim's dad. 'But mistakes happen.' He was smiling; he knew the woman hadn't meant to be a smuggler – and he was very pleased with Bella.

Bella was happy too. She wagged her tail again, and when Tim's dad nodded she walked on past the next line of people and their bags. She loved chewy treats, and she loved Matt patting and praising her. And most of all, Bella loved the game of sniffing.

About the Author

Wendy Orr was born in Edmonton, Canada, and spent her childhood in various places across Canada, France and the USA, but wherever she lived, there were lots of stories, adventures and animals. Once, when her family sailed to a new home, the dogs wore life-jackets, but the guinea pigs had to stay in their cages. When she grew up and had her own family, she still had cats, guinea pigs, rabbits and horses at different times – and always dogs. Her most recent dog is Harry, an occasionally naughty but always delightful poodle-cross that she adopted from the Lort Smith Animal Shelter. Harry had a very bad start to life and Wendy and her husband feel very lucky that he has come to live with them, and that they can all be happy together.

Wendy is the author of a number of award-winning books, including *Nim's Island*, *Nim at Sea*,

Mokie and Bik, *The Princess and her Panther*, *Raven's Mountain* and for teenagers, *Peeling the Onion*.

A few years after Wendy wrote *Nim's Island*, a film producer in Hollywood took the book out of the library to read to her son, and the next day emailed Wendy to ask if she could make it into a movie. Wendy said yes! They became good friends and Wendy had the fun of helping work on the screenplay, and learning that making a movie was even more complicated than writing a book.

Wendy Orr lives in Australia on the Mornington Peninsula in Victoria.